NEW DIRECTIONS 51

In memoriam
WAYNE ANDREWS
1913-1987

New Directions in Prose and Poetry 51

Edited by J. Laughlin

with Peter Glassgold and Griselda Ohannessian

 A New Directions Book

Unsolicited manuscripts must be accompanied by a self-addressed, stamped envelope and, in the case of translations, written permission from the foreign writer, publisher, or author's estate.

ACKNOWLEDGMENTS
Grateful acknowledgment is made to the editors and publishers of magazines in which some of the material in this volume first appeared; for Martin Bax, *Ambit* (London); for Joe David Bellamy, *The Ontario Review* (Copyright © 1984 by Joe David Bellamy); for Maclin Bocock, *The Southern Review* (Copyright © 1986 by Louisiana State University); for George Evans, *Origin* (Copyright © 1983 by the National Poetry Foundation) and *Scripsi* (Australia); for Gavin Ewart, *The Times Literary Supplement* (Great Britain); for James B. Hall, *New Letters* (Copyright © 1984 by The Curators of the University of Missouri); for James Laughlin, *In hui* (France).

Richard M. Bomstein's poems were first published in his privately printed collections *For the Sake of Argument* (Copyright © 1984 by Richard M. Bomstein) and *Footnoise* (Copyright © 1985 by Richard M. Bomstein) and are reprinted by permission of the author.

Manufactured in the United States of America
First published clothbound (ISBN: 0-8112-1033-2) and New Directions Paperbook 644 (ISBN: 0-8112-1034-0) in 1987
Published simultaneously in Canada by Penguin Books Canada Limited

New Directions Books are published for James Laughlin
by New Directions Publishing Corporation,
80 Eighth Avenue, New York 10011

CONTENTS

A MAN SIXTY

SHUSAKU ENDO

Translated by Lawrence Rogers

I'm not sleeping well these days, among other things; maybe it's age. Over the course of a night I have many dreams, each a separate entity, and as soon as I've had my dream I wake up. For a short time I lie awake in the dark, eyes wide open, absorbed by my inevitable death. I turned sixty this month.

I had this dream the other night. I was in a dark room. I was sitting across from the writer Ryunosuke Akutagawa. He sits with his arms folded, head bowed, wearing a threadbare grayish summer kimono. He utters not a word. Suddenly he stands up, pushes through the bamboo curtains behind him, and goes into the next room. I know that this adjoining room is the world of the dead, yet Akutagawa soon passes through the curtain again, coming back into the room I'm in. Then I woke up. After I awoke I wondered dully why I should now be having this morbid sort of dream so often. I could hear my sleeping wife's tranquil breathing beside me.

I would not, of course, tell my wife about the dreams I have been having. I doubt that it would interest her even if I did. It has been my intention over the years at home—it is curious for me to admit it—to wear the mask of the tolerably decent husband and father. Putting on the mask, however, does not really mean that I have made myself play a role foreign to me. This is because a part of my personality is instinctively amiable in dealing with others. And yet

1

the face of decent husband and father, of course, is not all there is
to me, for there is another face unknown to my family. No doubt
you can say that about any husband.

Every day at ten in the morning it is my custom to open up this
workroom—near Tokyo's Harajuku district—and enter my roughly
nine-foot-square room with its tightly drawn curtains. When I sit
down at my desk, strewn with papers, dictionaries, and books in
grand disorder, my face is now my own face, which need not trou-
ble itself about imposing on others. I am afraid that visage is as
morbid as the dreams I have every night. I sometimes suspect, as I
look into the mirror, that the Buddhist term Unenlightened Face
may refer to one such as mine. The downward-turned face of
Ryunosuke Akutagawa that appeared in my dream, a world that
seeks salvation while it is yet unable to discover the light.

That face is starting work on a novel. Having said that, I should
add that at sixty I no longer do much of the sort of work where one
is under the pressure of a deadline. What I'm doing now is a thor-
oughgoing rewriting of *The Life of Jesus,* a book published some
fifteen years ago, though I haven't decided yet which publisher will
put it out.

Reading my fifteen-year-old book is, as you might expect, unsatis-
fying. While I would not call it superficial, at forty-five years of age
I had not read the Bible with full understanding. There were many
passages where I relied on the interpretations of various Western
scholars and did not digest each and every word myself.

I had thought, for example, that the only conceivable reason why
Jesus was forsaken, not only forsaken but treated sadistically, per-
secuted, struck, spat upon, and then killed by people who only the
day before had welcomed him with open arms, was simple mob
psychology. Most certainly Jesus, who had preached the doctrine of
love, was killed as a political offender, yet I made no serious at-
tempt to ask why everyone should have wanted to persecute him.

As I reread the book I had written fifteen years earlier, this dis-
satisfaction confronted me on almost every page. Of course, it was
also in this tiny, humid workroom that, day by day, I wrote *The
Life of Jesus* fifteen years ago. (I cannot get any work done unless
I am sitting in a room about this size, curtains drawn even during
the day. A room with just the right darkness and just the right
humidity provides me with the sense of liberation of my mother's
womb.) I was optimistic then that the parade of misgivings and

questions that came to me in reading the New Testament would be dispelled within a decade and that I would no doubt be able to meekly accept everything. Yet ten years later, and even now, fifteen years later, at sixty, a sure inner peace of mind still eludes me, and now and again the intense hellfires of doubt flare up yet more wretchedly.

This small room has changed little over the last fifteen years. The desk and chair, the clock and table lamp and Chinese writing brush-stand on the desk are just as they were then. Several old maps that I had bought when I was a student in my twenties in Lyons are displayed in frames on the wall. My habit of writing with a 3B pencil, bent almost double over my desk, has not changed over the years. If I did not have my reading glasses now, however—unneeded when I was forty-five—I could not do any work. Not only have my eyes faltered, my body itself has declined over these fifteen years, nibbled and gnawed at by age, bite by bite. Years ago it was nothing for me to sit in this chair hour after hour. Now I suffer from an intensifying ache from my hips to my groin if I'm in the same position for two hours. I've had sciatica for the last three years.

When I leave my study at the usual time for my afternoon stroll to best the pain of the sciatica, I slip a pocket body warmer in my back pocket and put on a moderately heavy coat. Yoyogi Park and the building site and plaza of NHK, the government broadcasting service, are nearby, so I can stroll undisturbed by traffic.

These days, however, I go neither to Yoyogi Park, where young mothers bring their children to play, nor to the broadcasting company's plaza, where young people practice badminton. Instead, I head directly for the district fronting Meiji Shrine in Harajuku.

The fact is, there is a coffee shop called The Swan on a side street, and it has been my custom since the onset of winter to sit for close to an hour at a window there from three in the afternoon. I sit next to the window because I know that a little after three students from a girls' high school on their way home will come by to buy ice cream at the confectioner's across the street. I have observed that when they are together in a group they joke and clown around, and yet if one is walking along the street by herself, her awareness of others' stares is almost comical in its intensity. I find this amusing.

Occasionally several of the more wayward girls will come into the coffee shop. Their waywardness we can divine simply from their patronage of a coffee house—which their school doubtless forbids—in their school uniforms, but even an old man like me can somehow sense this from their language and from the fact that they have intentionally lengthened their skirts. They defiantly open the door of the coffee shop, casting a disdainful glance at the other students, and as they go by me my nostrils are assailed by the pungent smell that greets you when you step into the woods in spring. At first I thought it was the uniforms, but then I realized that it was not that but rather the body scent of girls of that age. They chat on with animation, their talk peppered with many strange words unintelligible to me. In time I understood that they called boys "betcho," menstruation "E.T.," and homework "debo." Their language is the language of boys; it is rough and abrupt, and at times they drop their verbs and simply string nouns together, in spite of which they seem to get their meaning across to one another.

Their faces, forbidden the use of make-up, are not without pimples, and their cheeks are blood-flushed red. Yet in their necks and faces I often sense the pain of living that the early spring woods are rich with, and usually lost by the time a woman reaches her mid-twenties, and I have sometimes winced in surprise in spite of myself.

I remember talking with an old fellow some twenty years ago. He was a scholar, an expert on woodblock prints. After giving his lecture at the university, he used to go home, put on a wig and blue jeans and dark sunglasses and—now disguised as a young man—go go-go dancing. I asked him why he did this, and he replied with a forced, embarrassed smile that the dance hall was in a basement and dark, and, besides, everyone was absorbed in their own frenetic dancing and did not realize he was an old man. Even teenage girls danced with him, he said.

"You know how the nape of the neck gets damp with sweat as they dance. They give off the faintest smell of sweat. There is something erotic about the smell of the sweat that older women don't have. I, uh, close my eyes and breathe in the scent to my heart's content."

I was still only forty or so when I talked with the old professor and not able to appreciate firsthand the sorrow and isolation of growing old. Now, however, having reached his age, I understand.

How it feels to close one's eyes and inhale the smell of a teenage girl's sweat. How it feels for one who soon must bid farewell to this life to try desperately to breathe in the smell of life at its zenith. I recall what he told me as I steal glances at the high-school girls from my seat by the window.

To what extent have they been aware of my gaze? Actually, these imps have seemed instinctively to know exactly what I am doing. Doubtless they are aware, but they go on talking, pretending not to know. And one day, with little real effort, I listened in on their conversation.

"Listen," said one girl, "he probably likes you too, Onami."

"I dunno," the other answered.

"How about sending him chocolates—on Valentine's Day. Then you could see how he responds."

The girl referred to as Onami was a narrowed-eyed youngster. She responded with a quick, cretinous smile. Her face, however, was the innocent face of a junior high-school student. She stood up without giving an answer and went to the restroom at the back of the shop.

"Look at that!" teased one of her friends at the table, "aren't we putting on airs. Miss Goody Two-shoes! She always acts like that, and even fools Mr. Matsuda."

Onami, going into the restroom, smiled quickly again, the upper half of her body still visible from behind the door, and shook her fist. This was an exchange and a gesture of no great moment to the girls, but I was struck for an instant by a feeling I was at a loss to describe.

Why should I have experienced such a feeling? At the time I had no idea. As I walked down the broad sloping street that skirts Yoyogi Park as it runs from Harajuku to my workplace, however, I sensed I had seen the episode of moments ago someplace else years before. I also sensed that I had experienced the same feeling then as well. Yet I did not know where. I opened the door of my study room savoring the impatience of one confronted with a scene out of one's dreams. When I sat down at my desk I remembered the confession of Stavrogin in a work by Dostoevsky. That was it! The behavior of the girl in the coffee shop was like that of the twelve-year-old girl Matryosha, assaulted by Stavrogin, the main character in *The Possessed*.

Stavrogin, knowing that her parents will be out, visits Matryosha's home one summer evening. He violates her. After the deed is done, she first fixes him in her gaze, her large eyes wide, then suddenly, with a look of contempt, threateningly shakes her fist at him. She leaves the room and goes to a small, chickencoop-like shed next to the outhouse, where she will hang herself. Stavrogin intuits what she is going to do, yet stays where he is, scrutinizing a tiny red spider crawling on a geranium leaf by the window.

Four years after the incident, when he is traveling in Germany, he dreams of a painting by Claude Lorraine. The work was itself based on a dream the painter had of a paradise on earth.

> Magnificent people lived there. They lived their days and nights in happiness, ignorant of sin. The woods were filled with the cheerful singing of the people. The sun rejoiced at the sight of its children and shone brilliantly over the islands and the sea. A wondrous dream. The most incredible amongst all the dreams that ever were. Yet it is precisely for this dream that all humanity offers up its life, the whole of its power, and it is for this it sacrifices all, for this it dies upon the cross and kills its prophets.

But in that instant Stavrogin saw facing him in the shining light, in the light of the earthly paradise, looking at him in contempt and shaking her little fist, the apparition of Matryosha, her eyes shining feverishly. He was stunned.

I first read this passage some forty years ago when I was a student. I had lodgings in Tokyo's Shinanomachi district, where I could hear the never-ending racket of the National Railway trains as they came into and left the nearby station. At the time I felt there was something indescribably ominous about Stavrogin. The act of violating an innocent, unsullied girl provoked in me disgust, and at the same time, curiosity. And now, most certainly, the toilet and the girl shaking her fist had resurrected my recollection of the Dostoevsky story.

Afterward I inevitably recalled this whenever I sat next to the window in The Swan and caught sight of the girl in the group from the girls' high school. The old man of sixty looks furtively at the girl of sixteen or seventeen. I cannot get the elderly scholar's story of long ago out of my mind. I am curious only about the girl whose language is slovenly, whose quick-smiling face is idiotic, and who therefore, more than any of the other girls, reminds me of the girl Matryosha, and whose expression betrayed her for the briefest instant.

My wife of many years comes over to my workroom once a week to clean up. On those days I assume a different countenance from when I am alone in my room. No, that's not the way to put it. To say that I revert to myself as I am at home is closer to the mark. That is because there nothing is forced, and I am without pretense or hypocrisy.

After we have lunch the two of us go out for a walk. I have never, however, taken her to The Swan, nor have I told her about the students from the girls' high school. Those things have nothing to do with our thirty years of life together. It is a warm winter this year, and as we walk along dodging the oncoming traffic, we enjoy the warmth of a mild sun on our shoulders.

We sit down on a bench in a corner of the NHK square. I watch the young people at their badminton practice in the distance. My wife is watching them too. I am pretty sure I know what she is thinking now. Many years ago—yes, it's been a long time—we were as young as those young people. We were going to the same university. Over some thirty-five years I have suffered from extended illness, we have gone abroad together, on occasion we have consoled one another, and hurt each other with the demands of our egos, experiencing, in short, the usual things common to married couples. And now we are perched on the bench like two little birds, the gentle rays of the sun falling on our backs and weighing drowsily on our eyelids.

When I was a student in France the concierge where I lived—an old man, and his wife—told me that they knew each other so well there was no need for words. I suddenly remembered what they had said. But having reached sixty I now realized that was not putting it right. Even man and wife do not know everything there is to know about each other. Were I to tell my wife that, however, I suspect she would merely respond with a pained expression. There is certainly no need at this point to torment a woman now grown old, her hair streaked with the gray she did not have when she was young.

"I'll be going now. Is that all right?"

"No problem. I should get back tonight around seven."

After she leaves my workroom once again becomes mine alone. Steam rises noiselessly from the electric stove. I rewrite the execution scene in *The Life of Jesus*. I try to recall Jerusalem's Old City where I took my wife three or four times to get a feeling for this scene. The town has changed since the time of Christ, yet the sense of the period still remains in the Old City. This town of alleyways befouled by donkey dung and urine, streets hemmed by dirty walls, twisting, dead-ended. Bronze plaques were set in the building walls: *Here Christ fell under the cross he was carrying. This was the site of the official residence of Pontius Pilate, who passed judgment on Christ.* Each time my wife came upon one of these, she would bow her head and pray, and I would follow her example. I prayed not out of hypocrisy but from honest feeling. I prayed from the bottom of the heart of the other me.

I could hear the commotion raised by the multitudes who had reviled Christ, who had stoned and spat upon him. That is what a mob is like. (Both during and after the war I had seen more of such mobs than I cared to.) They were the same people who had fanatically supported Christ only the day before. Why had they changed so radically? Fifteen years earlier I had written in my book:

> It was because they realized Jesus was a powerless man who could not bring their dream to realization. They knew this man was of no use in their dream of driving Rome from their country.

This interpretation is not erroneous. It is, however, what several scholars had said and is not a statement that I had distilled from my own experiences. Something was lacking.

The sun sets. I am relieved that it is now pitch-dark beyond the closed window curtains. It is almost seven o'clock when the pain in my hip starts and I at last make ready to go home. As I always do, I turn off the lights and check the gas burner.

My home is an hour from Tokyo by train, and the winter temperature is several degrees cooler than it is in the city. Thus the nights can be a bit unpleasant for someone with sciatica. That is not my only ailment. I had a certain amount of confidence in my health until the age of fifty-five, when I had surgery on my nose, and perhaps because of that my health abruptly changed for the worse. Suddenly I saw the loathsome face of age everywhere upon my flesh. I began to suffer from shortness of breath and vertigo, cold hands and feet, and one by one my teeth went bad.

For a while on the platform at the Harajuku train station there was a wall poster proclaiming "The Beautiful Mature Years," which featured two older actors, Ken Uehara and Mieko Takamine. You can rename old age "the mature years" if you like, but the reality is unchanged. At bottom there is just no way to age beautifully. That old age is brutally ugly I can verify simply by looking at my face and physique reflected in my mirror. Ugliness—the dingy, lifeless hair, the age spots on my skin—lies not simply in the face and body. Ugliness also comes from being as yet unvisited by tranquility and peace of mind in spite of those sixty years. I am sixty, yet still God does not give me these feelings: at night, between one dream and the next when I lie open-eyed in the darkness, the fear of death suddenly, abruptly assails me. The extinction of my flesh. No longer able to see the light of morning, the streets of the city, people moving about. Unable to smell the warm aroma of coffee. When I think of these things, my heart suffers pain poignant as a knife thrust. Where shall I breathe my last breath? When? I try not to think about it. I try to get to sleep quickly to escape the thought of it. The ugliness of age means to be unable to separate oneself from this despicable obsession.

On Sunday a corner of Yoyogi Park and the road adjoining it are filled with onlookers looking at the Shedders, those alienated young people who put on their curious clothes and do their group dancing. The onlookers intently watch the young men and women who have formed several circles and dance their bizarre dances in time to music from their cassette recorders. I am one of the onlookers. The Shedders are wearing long pink and white tunics, the sort that Koreans favor, and have rouged their cheeks, the boys as well as the girls. Each circle is different from the next and has its own leader, under whose guidance it dances. Nearby a Westerner busily grinds away on his 8mm camera. As I watch them dancing I recall wistfully how it was during the war when I was the age of these young men and women.

She is among the spectators. The girl who shook her fist threateningly at her friends in The Swan. The narrow-eyed girl with the idiotic smile who nonetheless still has a hint of schoolgirl innocence in her face, an innocence that reminded me of the violated Matryosha. She is not in her uniform today, wearing instead what appears to be a hand-knit sweater and a muffler.

I observed her carefully. She was watching the Shedders' movements with fascination, running her tongue over her upper lip. It was obvious from her expression that she very much wanted to join one of the circles, but the music soon stopped and the young people took a break, at which point she looked up and noticed me with a start.

"Well!" I said, affecting the familiar chuckle of a man who has just run across his favorite niece, "you live around here, do you?"

"By the Odakyu line station. What about you?"

Stalls selling broiled squid and hamburgers lined the street. When I asked her if she would like some coffee, she replied, hands under her muffler, that she would rather have a Coke. It was Sunday, and both Yoyogi Park and the NHK plaza were crowded with families out looking for sunshine, so we walked over to the bench my wife and I had sat on earlier. Just as I had with my wife, I now sat down on the bench with the girl. I handed her a bottle of Coke and a bag of popcorn. When she wore her school uniform her figure had seemed childlike to me, but now as I looked at her body under the tight-fitting sweater, I could see that her breasts were full, though an innocence remained in her narrow-eyed face and the mouth with its prominent eyeteeth. Looking at the running shoes with their slightly scuffed toes and her wash-worn sweater, I tried to visualize her apparently less-than-affluent home.

"*Ojisan,*" she began, using the word a young person uses for a man who is older, "does that interest you?"

" 'That'?"

"Y'know what I mean. The Shedders. They're just a bunch of hayseeds."

"But they are interesting, aren't they."

Coke bottle in hand, she turned to me with a look of contempt.

"Those hicks? What's so interesting about 'em?"

"What's interesting? Well, young girls intrigue me."

She fell silent, then looked up at me, her eyes upturned, as if to fathom my intentions. Near us five or six pigeons foraged endlessly for food, but suddenly took flight when a youth with a Walkman headset on and a boy on roller-skates, arms outspread, approached. She waited until they were far away.

"They're a lot of men like you, y'know." Her statement was muttered, sudden.

"How like me?"

"Adults interested in, you know, young girls."

"There're that many?"

"There's plenty. They call out to you when you walk along the street."

"To you kids? But they're middle-aged, aren't they?"

"Some are middle-aged, but some are old like you." Again she laughed contemptuously. Her teeth were schoolgirl white. A woman over twenty-five of course, would not have such teeth.

"You yourself were checkin' us out at The Swan, weren't you."

"What do you do when someone says something to you?"

"It's obvious, right, what a man has on his mind."

"Do you go with him, you and your friends?"

"Some do. They say even old men will buy you stuff and give you lots of money."

"What do they do for the money?"

"Up to C."

I asked what C meant and learned that among the students at the girls' high school, by and large, a kiss was A, petting was B, the ultimate stage being C. I had, of course, read something of the sort in the weekly news magazines, but to hear this disclosure directly from the lips of this young girl gave it singular freshness. I stole another look at her maturing body.

"Do you, ah, do that sort of thing?"

"I don't, no."

"What about your friends, the ones who go to The Swan?"

"They don't. But I know someone else who will do it if you give her money."

Her answer rang false. It just might be that this girl was that "someone else." Her tone of voice, however, suggested she could be telling the truth.

"That sort of thing, you know, one ought not do it."

"Right," she responded, disinterest suddenly in her voice. It was an inflection that questioned the proffering at this point of conventional adult advice.

"What's your name?" I asked.

"Namiko."

"Will you come here again next Sunday?"

"I dunno. I might if I'm bored."

After I returned to my workroom that day I tried to work on my draft of *The Life of Jesus* in the room with its tightly drawn curtains, but I could not get her and the conversation we had had out of my mind. It was not, of course, that I harbored a sexual interest in the girl. Nonetheless, I was intensely curious as to why she had suddenly started off on that conversational tack with an old man like me. Was it her intention to taunt me? Was she intending to do me a favor? Or did she, in fact, want to seduce me?

Naturally, I did not anticipate making a misstep with a girl more than forty years my junior. I had reached the age where—in contrast to my younger days—creating turmoil in my life was now more bother than it was worth, and besides, I considered myself a Christian of sorts.

And so it was that on the following day I went back to The Swan to savor my customary pleasure of surreptitiously watching young girls, my mind at a kind of peace with itself. Unfortunately, they were not there. The next day, and the day after, I took my seat by the window and waited for Namiko to appear with her friends. Four or five days later when I opened the coffee shop door she and her group were deep in conversation. Namiko ignored me even though she glanced at me, but this, to the contrary, made me think she was quite aware of me, since she was laughing and cutting up more than usual.

"She said she'd do anything if a man bought her some clothes."

"Awesome!"

"Could you go that far?"

She was at the center of things today, talking in a tone that may or may not have been meant to be taken seriously. It may be vanity on my part, but it seemed to me she was doing this because she wanted me to hear what she had to say on this particular subject. However, it could also have been taken as joking, depending on how you took it.

"It depends on the clothes."

"Not the clothes, but who's giving them to you."

"If it were a guy like Michael Jackson I'd settle for something cheap."

"You said it!"

It was then that for the first time she gave me a searching look. She was clearly watching my reaction. Then she casually changed the direction of the conversation.

"How about going to see the Shedders Sunday?"

"Those nerds!? No way! You go and watch them?"

"I was bored the other day, so I went."

This time she did not turn her gaze in my direction. Nonetheless, I took this as a signal from her.

On Sunday I panted my way up the hill in the park where the Shedders were making their circles. Years ago I had had lung surgery and had been forced since then to walk at a leisurely pace lest I run out of breath, and yet here I was panting and striding along in a great hurry, and when I suddenly realized what I was doing I grinned wryly in spite of myself. The smell of broiled squid and the sound of cassette music wafted down on the breeze from the top of the hill, and again today the dancers were surrounded by onlookers.

I looked for her, but she was not there. My self-satisfaction was shattered and my pride wounded as I concluded I had been bamboozled by a girl no older than my youngest daughter. I excoriated myself harshly: At your age! What do you want? Yet I myself did not know what I wanted.

Nonetheless, hands in my pockets, I absent-mindedly watched the Shedder youngsters in their Korean-style clothes as they clapped their hands, lifted their legs, clung to each other, and circled about. The dull, nasty sciatic ache in my hip was spreading. As usual I felt my aged, now-unlovely flesh in that pain, and I stared at the Shedders with envy.

Someone poked me. I turned around and there she was, her eyes narrowed in laughter.

"I was sure you'd be here."

"You were?" I was quickly forgetting my hip pain.

We sat ourselves down on last Sunday's bench, and I gave her a bottle of Coke. It was just like the previous Sunday: children on roller-skates and young men with Walkmans at their ears strolling about, forcing me to recall myself during the war.

"D'ya like music?"

"Yes, I do."

"Who d'ya like?"

"Who? Oh, Bach and Mozart and . . ."

"You don't like pop music?"

I shook my head and told her I didn't know too much about it.

"Sure wish I could buy a whole bunch of records." Her head was bowed and she muttered, as though talking to herself.

"A whole bunch."

I looked at that bowed head's full, healthy cheeks. There was not one wrinkle, not even around the eyes. Unlike me, this girl had many years ahead of her. Her life lay before her. And in contrast to her there was me. She dug at the ground with her muddied tennis shoe. I knew from the look of those shoes that she did not have pocket money to buy records.

"I'd really like to buy a Michael Jackson record."

She seemed to be angling for money for a record.

"You want a record that badly?"

"I do. A record and clothes and a Walkman."

She continued to dig up the dirt with the toe of her shoe, head still bowed. It could well be she had enticed middle-aged men who had accosted her before with this sort of roundabout approach, or maybe this was the first time, maybe she was speaking in complete innocence.

"Well," I asked her half-jokingly, "what if I were to buy you records or clothes, would you do what your friend does?"

She looked up at me and gave me that quick, narrowed-eyed smile. The idiotic smile could as well have concealed shy embarrassment as signaled consent or her acceptance of my question as fun at her expense. I could see her eyeteeth when she smiled. It could have been a smile totally ignorant of life or one grossly obscene. This grinning face, neither childlike nor adult, chilled me to the bone. Suddenly it struck me that a single utterance of mine could well determine this girl's future. *Tell you what. I'll give you the money. In return, I want you to go out with me twice a month.* That simple statement from me could, in due time, sow the seeds of distrust toward men and toward love. Me—sixty years old. A seventeen-year-old student at a girls' high school. This youngster has a long life ahead of her. I have little left to me now. Yet it is possible that I would be the first to leave his mark upon her. The satisfaction and sense of control were too strong, and I left the words unsaid in spite of myself.

It was then that I noticed the dusk sky. The rays of the winter sun broke radiantly through a gap in the clouds directly over the Setagaya and Meguro districts of the city. As I looked at the blaze of light, the picture of paradise in Stavrogin's confession suddenly came back to me.

> Magnificent people lived there. They lived their days and nights in happiness, ignorant of sin. The woods were filled with the cheerful singing of the people. The sun rejoiced at the sight of its children and shone brilliantly over the islands and the sea. A wondrous dream. The most incredible among all the dreams that ever were.

I stood up, the imminent suggestion that we go somewhere left unsaid. We walked out to the sidewalk and went our separate ways, nonchalantly waving goodbye to each other.

For all my nonchalance, however, several nights later I had the following dream. I was in a hotel room I had used to write in years earlier. I went into the bathroom and took off my clothes. The dressing room mirror reflected back to me my thinning hair, my face with its age spots, my age-ravaged body. I stood purposefully before the mirror, surprised by an aging that went beyond reality, then carried away by a masochistic impulse, clownishly stuck out my tongue at my face in the mirror and laughed. It was not just a laugh. I intentionally emitted a loathsome chickenlike cackle.

My dream abruptly ended. When I drifted off again, I was holding down a girl who was thoroughly repulsed by me. It was Onami. She was desperately turning her head from side to side to escape my wet mouth. The more she thrashed about to get away, the more I wanted to hurt her. I rubbed my body—senescence itself—against her breasts and thighs and eagerly fouled her plump cheeks and eyelids, still retaining their innocence, with an old man's saliva. I was not acting out of lust but from an impulse that drove me literally to violate her life.

I woke up. A smoldering emberlike something still burned crimson within me. I read somewhere that dreams are manifestations of desires that we refuse to admit to, and the dream I had just had was undeniably such a dream.

All was still, save for the sound of my wife's breathing as she lay asleep beside me. Eyes shining in the darkness, I ruminated this most recent dream like some beast in the wilds. The envy a man of sixty who would soon enough leave this world harbored toward a girl who would go on living in it had created the dream. The enmity of a life on the wane toward a student in a girls' high school who is full of life was at its heart. I knew that monstrous things from my unconscious had taken shape and shown themselves to me: a despicable attachment to what was already lost, a sadism intent on hurting her full, rich being. The man who has written *The Life of Jesus* holds within his heart such feelings yet again.

My wife slept on right beside me, her breathing steady and peaceful. I thought about the difference in the soundness of her sleep and mine. To some people God gives peace with age, and to others He gives fear of death, fierce attachment to life, envy of those who will go on living, and unseemly struggle.

Today I once again went for a walk with my wife, who had come to tidy up my writing room. It was a warm day, so my hip wasn't bothering me, and as we walked along I even took off the muffler I had wrapped around my neck as a precaution. My wife was talking about her niece, who had married two weeks before. She said the couple had gone to California on their honeymoon.

"It's so different from when we got married, isn't it."

"It was tough for us even to go as far as Nara."

The signal was about to change, so the two of us stopped, waiting together patiently side-by-side like two birds on a perch. Both my wife and I were now leery of making a run for it as we had years before.

Again today we sat down on the bench at the NHK plaza. It wasn't Sunday, so neither the music of the Shedders nor the commotion of sightseers was to be heard. My wife folded her hands over the handbag in her lap.

"They say they're going to live with his parents for the time being. Setchan apparently doesn't think much of that."

"Nobody thought anything about it in the old days," I answered. "Having your own place when you were newlyweds was too much to hope for."

This was the same bench I had sat on last Sunday with the girl.

My wife, of course, knew nothing of this. And as had happened then—a corner of the sky where the sun shone brightly. The picture of paradise that Stavrogin saw. The Kingdom of God that Jesus told of.

"Look! Where the sun is shining! Doesn't that remind you of Jerusalem seen from the Mount of Olives?"

"I wonder," my wife answered, "the city there was more whitish, I think."

I nodded as she talked on, but I was thinking of the draft of *The Life of Jesus* I had left on my desk. I discover the figure of an old man in the mob that is reviling Jesus, who has been taken into custody. A docile Jesus, covered with blood and dirt, is being led away. He does not resist. His eyes are downcast. In front of the old man, however, he lifts his head. His eyes as he looks at the old man are crystal clear, as clear as a young girl's. The old man flinches before Him whose purity is everlasting. His envy is provoked. He spits upon Jesus before he realizes what he is doing. The old man must at least humiliate his flesh, as I had done to the girl in my dream.

A young housewife passes in front of the bench, glances quickly at us, and gives us a friendly smile. Obviously she considers us an old couple who have passed through all of life's trials and have now achieved a life of tranquility. And she thinks she would like to be like us someday.

BIOLOGY

JOHN ALLMAN

1

                              There is only this
        steel bridge rusted out

            fishermen's
    flat-bottomed
    boats upended
    on a muddy slope
                              swans congregating
                              on Muscoot reservoir
          the western hill
                you call your mountain

              this overcast
                    day's
              blank
    Pepsico
       building
            squaring off a rounded
                    shoreline   stone and glass
                          supplanting
                    trees
                       stripped of bark by white-tail

                deer   there is only
                              our blood
                  converging   our mixed
                  inheritance of dirt from Irish
farms
the fields of Krk

                            eons of insensate
                                          stone
                      angular unconformities
                                        of Being
                          imitating granite and
                            basalt   heaved
                      into a dream of
                            Adriatic air

we are
here   we are here
in the smallest fold
          of unborn
            leaves

          turning off the road
          behind our house
watching a haggard hawk
                  swoop to her
                  survival

a wound occurring
among pines
          in there the small
      scream   the sudden
                  death

              the cud
            of a violent cosmos
              spewed into the eventual
                  coolness of a peony's
              interior
                  the scarlet peony here
                  simply to be here

again   as the yellow
                          finch is here
                     on our wide-mesh fence
                     that protects New Guinea impatiens
               from the dog   the finch
                          here above the hidden
                          blackness of the cat
                          in the cool hostas

          the finch singing
where I dig up plantain
          from the driveway
                              where sparrows scour
          the naked stone
for seed   dandelions rooted between
                     broken cinder blocks
                          and brick   the beige
                     spider suddenly the exact color
                          we have painted
                          our garage
          the finch and his
          mate   flying the curve of a sine wave
                    up
          into the storm-broken
          branch of a maple   into

                                   opportunity

                     above the cat
                     and spider

2

Opposite Daufuskie Island

                          Calibogue
                          Sound yields
                    to the open sea
                              exhausted

          where we harvest
          a low tide's

                    display
                                    the sea cucumber opening
                                    her tentacles
                                        in the plastic cup we fill
                                    with water
                sister to the hydra

                    listen
            listen   we might
                                        amble in the twilight
                        on jointed legs
our skeletons external   turning knee-deep
                                in the shallows of the sand bar
                    we might radiate a more exact
            symmetry   extrude a pharynx
                                    in the long wash of sunset

                                our tanned
                            faces uplifted
                            to receive the shadows
                            of pelicans
the bony parts
and the soft parts   in the green capacity
                                    of sea lettuce   making
                                        selves from
                                            light and the salty
                                    secretions of coral
                            and the bequeathed movement of the first
                                    alga into a puddle
                                that dried into land
                                        where we might have been
                                blue-green
                                    or brown or red

                plants
            hungry for the touch
                        of beetle legs
                            on trigger hairs
            snapping shut spiny lobes
            while we slowly digest

        death and grow
        alert to the purposes
          of hardness   the long projection
                  of the horseshoe crab's
                      spine

    like a weapon

           a deadly dart

 that we see it
  dig
into the
 sand to
 upright itself

             its carapace later
             a thin
             crackling papyrus
             in the dog's jaws

what would we do clinging and sedentary in a moist habitat
what would we think facing each other across minute distances
like the barely distinguishable parts of moss or the chipped
pinecone that has come to rest beneath pink and yellow zinnias

what amphibian lurch of the backbone takes us into the compost
where the tortoise lays her eggs and the small cadavers of
toads have been flung by the mower's blades what would we assert as
ours as desire is ours as the distinct cavity of the mouth is ours

3

        We have come

to this
particular
 strip
 of Sea Pines Plantation

             not to forget the twin
             bridges into Charleston
             and the fright of traveling
             thin steel over so much
              harbor

not to forget the ladies
waving sweet
grass into baskets
among cut flowers
in front of a circular
church

not to be able to say
a Gullah sentence and
know nothing of black women
who live by quick twinings of their fingers
who walk on sand
between washed-up
reeds and razor-sharp
burrs   carrying life
on the surface of pain

not to believe the blind
life of plants
could be
unthinkingly
ours

not to be
automatic
as filter-feeding
mosquito larvae
beating a current
into their
gullets

the earthworm
grinding particles
in its gizzard
not to know
the backward-curved teeth of the snake
holding down what is already a bulge in the body
though everywhere
a need to take
within

to have out-there

become

where will begins
as the hunger of oxygen
entering blood *whispering*
through the spiracles
of grasshoppers
into the stomata of shade-loving

trees

the action of any orifice
a sentience *a decision*
selection a kind of

pleasure

in momentum

the way we drove
to Bogue Island
and watched the lightning's
jagged plunge
sever the sky
to make our flooded
route rich in ozone

felt it entering
our pores
when we parked at Starvin' Marvin's
letting the sky carry its load
of darkness south from Hatteras
as if there had to be just so much
of it out there in the distance
to shade the cornfields
to move us closer
to each other   to balance
light and salt
in the clear lymph
that flows
between the heart's
pulse and the first
entry of something
into a wound   that was the sky
itself

that was the white-capped water of Atlantic
Beach
and the next day's clear weather
through Emerald Isle   the gouged woods
                    where condominiums
                proliferated
                        like organisms

and we talked of sulfur dioxide
used to kill the wild yeasts
that spoil wine   we sang our road
                            songs
        spilled the last coffee
            from a broken thermos

    felt the air
moving against us
            twisting through the vents
            sliding along the outer
                    surface of our
                            human
        volume

4

    Home
here it is
home   tiered slope of orange cosmos and white phlox
again   again
  the swollen pods of sweet
                william   long-necked
                        succulents   low-lying
                                blue
                ageratum along the slate walk

                    nothing

nothing
calls in dialect
so truly

as the wood thrush
          marking his particular
      tree
       his thin border
      like our
Dogwood Lane between
a neighbor revving
his open-throated
Trans-Am and me
hurtling on the tractor
downhill behind the peach trees
          all this roaring
each side of a street   all this singing
                          from the mulberry tree struggling up
              between Douglas firs

          all this counterpoint
of bird and bird
                    magnolia and mimosa
            the separate tangles
            of caged harmonies   of blown
blossoms and just emerging puffs
of scarlet   up there in the mimosa something like
sea anemones   the humming-bird darting across her
                          habitat
              into the dilated dusk
              of our eyes

where the Japanese beetles fall into a plastic bag
duped by synthetic mating scent   by the pheromone
                          that brings them
              copulating in the peach-colored roses
                    where I pluck them in pairs
                          crack them between thumb
                                  and forefinger
              in this August
            afternoon
            when I would seek the ants that
              stroke aphids

to milk for their
honeydew

I would see the round dance
and the waggle dance
of bees   I would tell you
just how distant
our food is from the hive
how many meters
my instinct travels
to attract
your
touch

where you tie up
wandering
morning-
glory's
mauve trumpets

THE BACK WAY TO FANTASYLAND

ALAN M. BROWN

It is at a party near Culver City. Alice meets Sam, is introduced by a mutual friend in front of the buffet, underneath a poster of Gene Kelly, Donald O'Connor, and Debbie Reynolds in yellow rain slickers.

"You have eyes like a chameleon's," she tells him right away, and it is true—his eyes are very round and shiny. The lids are almost translucent. But when Alice reaches up to stroke them, Sam backs up, stumbles, to avoid her touch.

Later, they sit together on the wooden lawn swing by the rose bushes, sip bourbon. It is an evening in early autumn, and the smell from the roses, from all of the flowers, is thick and strong. There are Japanese lanterns strung from the fruit trees; the white lights inside of them illuminate the lemons and limes like Christmas ornaments.

"I live in Palms," Alice tells Sam. "It's very close to here, practically down the block. I have a small house. And you?" she asks with apparent interest.

Sam lives at the Dunes, he explains to Alice, an RV park in Newport Beach. There is electricity to hook up to. Gas. Showers. "It's only seven dollars a night," Sam says, "and it's right on the ocean." Sam lives in a Winnebago that belonged to his parents. They left it for him when they moved away. Sam used to live with his parents, he lived in their home in Newport Beach until they traded houses with a couple from Mexico City. "Just like that," he says, snapping his fingers. Now there are two strangers in his parents' house. They invited Sam to stay on, they said he could keep his own room. The woman even called him "son." "But it just felt weird," Sam says, "I just couldn't do it. Besides, I like living in the Winnebago."

"Oh, yes, it must be wonderful," Alice beams at Sam. "You must have such a feeling, a feeling of freedom."

"I guess," Sam agrees. Sam is a janitor, works for the school district. He spends most of his time wandering the halls of his old elementary school, his old high school. Most of his teachers are still there, he tells Alice.

Alice is a secretary for a corporation of psychiatrists in Westwood, a job she inherited from her mother, who retired last year. Before that she did temporary work. But she is considering going back to school, thinking of finishing up her degree.

Alice looks up at Sam, smiles up at him with great enthusiasm. Alice is a California blonde. She is tan and very pretty, Sam notices, and surprisingly strong-looking. "Tomorrow is Saturday," she says in a voice buoyed up with bourbon and romance. "Saturday. Are you doing anything tomorrow? We could go somewhere."

Sam is caught off guard. His glass is empty, and what he is thinking is that he would like to get up off the swing and go and find the bourbon bottle. Instead, though, "Nothing at all. I'm not doing anything. Sure, I guess we could could go somewhere. We could take the Winnebago. Where would you like to go?"

Alice claps her hands together. "I've never been in a Winnebago before." Sam is confused; he is not used to enthusiasm. "I know, we can go to Disneyland," Alice suggests. "I absolutely love Disneyland, and I haven't been there in over a year."

"I suppose. If that's what you'd like to do," Sam nods. "Sure. Disneyland it is, then." He takes both of their empty glasses and goes in search of the bourbon.

Alice is up before dawn, and by seven she is on the freeway, on her way to meet Sam at the Dunes. On the way to Disneyland, she expresses great interest in the Winnebago. While Sam drives, she sits in the front passenger seat, at the kitchen table, on the edge of the overhead bed. Alice opens the cupboards, the tiny refrigerator, the closet, pulls back the shower curtain. She runs her hands over every surface and coos like a bird. "It's darling. Really it is. Just like a miniature house on wheels," she tells Sam. "Oh, I'd give anything to go on a long trip in here. We shouldn't stop at Disneyland, we should just keep right on going. Wouldn't you love to take this all the way to the Grand Canyon? Or to Mexico. We could drive all the way to the Yucatan if we wanted to."

At Disneyland, Sam takes Alice on all of the mountain rides: Space Mountain, Thunder Mountain, The Matterhorn. They shoot through cool, dark tunnels, where Alice squeezes Sam's arm tightly with both of her hands, and then out into the hot sunlight. On Thunder Mountain, they are supposed to pretend that the roller coaster is really an old steam locomotive, and as they careen through an abandoned mine shaft there is a simulated earthquake. Giant boulders break loose from the ceiling and crash menacingly down toward Alice and Sam. Alice screams and throws her arms around Sam's neck. Sam wonders if it might not be a real earthquake. Then, like a film run in reverse, the boulders fly back up and disappear into the roof. As the train hurtles down the last steep track, their car runs right through a small waterfall. The spray is refreshing, but now Alice's shirt is wet, soaked even, in the front. So, when she comes back from the restroom, she insists on tamer rides. She takes Sam on the Mad Hatter Tea Cups, through Snow White's Secret Cave, then up in Captain Hook's pirate ship. On this last ride, they fly into a nursery: three children sleep peacefully guarded by a big, furry sheepdog, while Peter Pan's shadow stretches mischievously across their beds. Alice and Sam's pirate ship sails out the window and over London chasing after a shimmering yellow light. It is Peter Pan's fairy, Tinkerbell, and as Alice and Sam approach her, as their little ship dips down over the islands and mermaid-filled lagoons of Never-never Land, Sam thinks that Tinkerbell's beating wings sound exactly like a hornet's.

On the next ride, they sit in comfortable theater seats while the stage revolves around them. This is a history of America through the nation's songs. Alice leans her head on Sam's shoulder. Sam enjoys being out of the hot sun, but he can't understand why everyone is applauding the mechanical animals. "This is taking anthropomorphism too far," he whispers to Alice in the middle of the show. Then, "They're machines, these people are clapping for fucking machines," he tells her.

"I'm sorry," Alice tells him when the show is over. She rests her hand lightly on his knee in an oblique caress. "It used to be a good ride. I always thought it was so much fun. I guess I just haven't been here in a while, that's all." They leave Tomorrowland, and Sam follows Alice through a maze of crowded paths.

"This is the back way to Fantasyland, I'm sure of it," she says. "I know my way around here. I mean, I was born only fifteen miles away." When they stop for ice cream sundaes, Alice runs over to the Polaroid Camera Shop on Main Street, U.S.A. She returns with a borrowed camera and insists that Sam pose with a tall, floppy-eared dog who whispers to Sam as Alice focuses, "Nice chick you got, buddy. Wish I could get the hell out of this crummy dog suit and meet some myself."

"My parents brought me here the day Disneyland opened," Alice tells him, the tall dog with the red vest. Goofy. "It was wonderful. Actually, I don't remember much, I was too little. But I just know it was fabulous. Can you imagine, the first day it opened?"

"Arf," is all the dog says to her. "Arf, arf, arf." He pats her on the ass and walks away.

Sleeping Beauty strolls by dressed in a long velvet cloak. "Poor thing, she must be awfully hot," Alice says to Sam, who is not listening. Later, they stand at an outdoor theater in Frontierland to watch a live show with real singers and dancers. The performers sing the Davy Crockett theme song. From the television show. Alice remembers and whistles along. Mickey and Minnie Mouse and two giant squirrels appear on stage wearing coonskin caps, and they wheel out Dumbo the Elephant on an enormous cart. Everyone dances except for Dumbo, who is too big to dance.

Back at Alice's house, a small house in Palms, Sam frightens her dog. "It's your beard," Alice explains. "He isn't used to seeing a man with a beard." Her dog, a Chihuahua, is barking and running wildly around the room and panting, and it doesn't stop, doesn't hold still for a moment. "Isn't he adorable?" Alice wants to know. "Like a hummingbird," she says.

Alice has no food in her house at all, only tea bags and a box of stale sugar donuts. But her mother lives just two houses down the street, so they go over there for dinner. Alice doesn't like her mother, she explains to Sam, doesn't like living so close to her, but her mother will baby-sit the dog, will take in her laundry, will come in when Alice is out and clean her house. Her mother serves them

German sausage steamed in beer. "It's October," she tells Sam. "There's a big holiday now in Germany, the Oktoberfest. The lady at the deli talked me into buying them. I'm such a pushover." She puts toothpicks on the table and hot mustard. "Dig in, kids," she says.

Later, Alice leaves her dog with her mother. She and Sam go out to a bar that Alice says is supposed to have good music. There is a piano player, and Alice sends him over a glass of white wine with a request to play "Raindrops Keep Falling on My Head." When they finally leave the bar it is two o'clock in the morning and there is a young man selling books on the sidewalk. The books are stacked in neat piles on a card table. "What is it?" Sam asks the man.

"It's my novel," the man announces loudly. "It's only two dollars. I had it printed up myself." He holds up a copy for Sam to examine. "See."

"How's business?" Sam wants to know.

"Sold forty already tonight. I make twenty-five cents on each copy."

"Why that's wonderful." Alice feels sorry for the young man, sorry for anyone who has to sell anything on the street in the middle of the night. So she gives him two dollars. But what she can't understand is, "Why don't you let the bookstores sell your book?"

The young man is clearly disturbed by this question, and he almost shouts his answer at her. "I don't have the time. I don't have time to waste on bookstores and besides, they're not interested in me, they're only interested in making money. Everybody knows that." Then, in a quieter voice, "Would you like me to inscribe it for you?"

"For Alice," she tells the young man. And then she spells it for him.

"It would be such fun," Alice says. "Like camping out on my own street."

But Sam refuses Alice's suggestion to spend the night in the Winnebago with him. "It's awfully uncomfortable," he explains. "Besides," he motions to the RV, "there's something wrong with the sink, and I'll probably be up half the night working on the pipes." He smiles at Alice and turns away. "I'll see you in the morning."

But Sam does park his Winnebago in Alice's driveway that night, and in the morning he goes into her house to shower. Sam carries his own soap dish, a towel. Then, because there is no food, they decide to go out for breakfast. They drive to a delicatessen in Beverly Hills where they have to wait an hour for a table. Sam buys a hard roll and a Danish, a cup of coffee over the counter. He sits down on the sidewalk in front of the restaurant. Alice is embarrassed and waits inside. "He might call our name," she tells Sam. "The man might call our name, and we wouldn't hear him from outside. We'd lose our table." Expensive cars pull up to the curb every few minutes, and people dressed in tennis clothes and jogging suits get out. When Alice and Sam finally get a table near the kitchen, this is what Sam orders for breafast: a "Hollywood," which is a hot corned beef and cole slaw sandwich on rye bread; a side of potato salad; an apple strudel with whipped cream; two large glasses of iced tea with a half of a lemon. Alice has coffee, scrambled eggs, and lox.

Sam tells Alice that it is time for him to head home. "I guess I'd better head on down to the Dunes," is how he puts it. But Alice suggests a ride on the Goodyear Blimp first. She takes out her wallet and shows Sam her Goodyear Blimp Club card. She has been on the blimp many times before, she tells him; she knows the man who runs it. She only has to make one phone call so she can check and see if it is all right, if the blimp is flying today, and if they can get on.

"Sure," Sam agrees. "Why not. I mean, hell, I've never been up in a blimp before. Why shouldn't we go?"

They stop in Venice on their way; Sam wants to see the roller skaters. They walk along the street and look in shop windows. Alice takes Sam into a gallery in Santa Monica she says is owned by Faye Dunaway, but Faye Dunaway is not there. "It's Sunday," Alice reasons. "She probably doesn't come in on Sundays." It is a warm day, they walk on the beach for a while. There are children building sand castles. "They're too near the water," Alice worries. "They should build them further up the beach so the tide won't wash them away." There are surfers sitting on their boards waiting for the waves. There are sailboats.

"Nice day for a swim," Sam observes.

"Oh, I've never been in the water in my life," Alice says. "Sometimes I bring my dog down and he goes in. He just loves it. But I've never been in myself. I'm afraid of the ocean."

Up in the blimp, Alice and Sam float out over Venice, out toward the open sea. Alice looks down, and she imagines that she can actually see the roller skaters and bicycle riders along the beach path. "We can go back to my house later," Alice looks at Sam, says cheerfully, "I can call my mother and ask her to have some dinner made. We can pick up some wine on the way." She hooks her arm in his, leans her head on Sam's shoulder. "You can park your Winnebago in the driveway again tonight. I don't mind, really. I think it's kind of fun. I can make tea and bring it out, and we can have a pajama party."

But Sam is not listening to her. Sam is looking straight out, out to the west. Alice suddenly feels that the blimp is really nothing but empty space, a huge silver cloth wrapped around a big empty space. She feels that she is being carried aloft by something that is not real, is not really there. Alice looks out the window, out the window of the Goodyear Blimp. She follows the sky straight down until it meets the ocean, and then she looks out across the endless gray mass below her. "Oh, Sam, look at the ocean, look at the waves," she says. "Isn't it beautiful?"

Sam looks down, looks at the sea. But they are not, in fact, looking at the sea, he realizes. They are looking at the fog.

A PATIENT OF DR. RYCROFT'S

GAVIN EWART

Today I am feeling comatic.
After a long night with Kit.
But all love is infantilistic
and even reactionary men
have no sense of structure—
even the most sensitive are incapable
of lasting personal relationships.
I regard all sex as masturbatory,
there's no point in kissing or "foreplay."

I have my language, you have yours.
A lowerarchy is a hierarchy viewed from above.
You laughed when you asked me
"Were you annoyed?"
and I answered "Annoyed? I was paranoid!"
Suffixes, prefixes? Who fixes them? I fix them.
There's iron in irony, although you smile.
Socrates? How does he come into it?

I don't understand metaphors,
semaphores and meaningless signals.
"Getting something off my chest"
means a bra or a boyfriend.
Things are things, and not other things.

You're surprised I call them "lovers"—
I have so many of them.
Most, you say, would mistrust, distrust
such casual encounters. I have no fear,
once a teenage pillion rider on a wall of death.
Just as I have no social shyness.

At 10 I decided to be Shakespeare, and a ventriloquist.
At 17 I wrote a poem identical with one of Verlaine's
and a melody identical with one by Rachmaninoff.
I could have been a great ballerina.
I have telepathic powers.
Freud, you say—"sexual overestimation of the ego."

But I have my effigies, and my own theory.
"Psychically real internal figures."
I worked it out myself,
with the help of two books,
one by Reik and one by Reich.
I want to be a child analyst.

Distelligent, sensationful, miswanted—
you smile at my vocabulary—but I still love cats.
If there are "love-objects"
in this world, they are cats.
They are overstanding.
All mothers are sadistic.

I am beautiful, and an actress.
I also believe I can find a way to be immortal.

L'ABECEDRIEN DE LA LUBRICITE[*]

JAMES LAUGHLIN

Si tu le permets, je veux prendre ton *arrière-train* pour rejoindre
    Henri Miller à Dijon

Je veux déguster ton *artiche* comme les feuilles d'un artichaut sauce
    hollandaise

Stupéfait de luxure, je prendrai ta *baba* au rhum Jamaica

Dans le costume de Monsieur Hulot je descendrai de ma cabine à
    roues pour me plonger dans ton *baigneur*

Je suis l'avocat de ton *bavard,* je te défendrai bien, tu n'iras pas au
    cachot

Quant aux *brioches,* je préfère les croissants, mais s'il s'agit des
    tiennes, elles me conviennent

Quand j'étais le plus petit à table on voulait toujours me donner le
    croupion du dindon; maintenant que je suis star de cinéma j'ai
    de plus grandes exigences

Mon enfance était vraiment dure; ma mère faisait fumer mon *dargif*
    à coups de sa brosse à cheveux; je ne te veux pas comme
    maman

Derechef je dis, je suis grand lecteur mais pas hypocrite; je suis
    pingre de ton *derche*

C'est vrai que la police tient mon dossier à jour, mais je ne suis pas
    dangereux; puisque tu ne portes que des pantalons de ski je ne
    pense pas que tu aies un slip à *dossière*

[*] N. d. E.: L'auteur a tenu à ce que soit respectée la manière dont il
s'exprime en français et dont il use de l'orthographe français.

Je dois admettre que je ne sais pas grand'chose des *entremichons* mais les lignes de ton corps sortent d'un dessin du Tintoret

C'est dans le *Faubourg* St. Germain que souvent je te vois avec ton amie Oriane de Guermantes; tu portes aussi des pantoufles rouges

Qui était le *Père Fouettard?* Je pourrais écrire sa biographie de toutes pièces mais ça me prendrait du temps. J'espère que ça n'a rien à faire avec les fouets; je ne vais jamais te faire de mal

Ne t'inquiéte pas de ton *gagne-pain;* je m'en chargerai afin que tu n'aies jamais besoin de te défendre comme ces pauvres filles dans l'histoire de Momo et Madame Rosa

Une *miche,* ça sonne comme une niche, qui est jolie, mais aussi comme une mouche, qui ne l'est pas. Alors je préfère la précédente. Quant aux niches, j'aime à la folie la niche de gauche de Bérénice quand elle essaie de la mettre dans son verre à vin.

On ne peut rien faire avec les *mouilles* qui ne soit pas, à mon avis, assez crasseux et dégeulasse, par exemple se torcher

Est-ce imbécile de dire qu'une paire de *noix* est belle? chacun à son goût; il y a des gens qui aiment les mordre, je le sais

Oui, je suis con comme un *panier* mais ce n'est pas toi qui m'as rendu idiot

On dit en anglais qu'on est "hoist with one's own *pétard";* ça arrive quand on se met en colère pour un rien

Le *pétoulet* est une rara avis qui habite les jungles lontaines de L'Amazonie et jouit d'un lien symbiotique avec des fourmis; il n'y en a pas en France sauf dans les livres pornographiques

Quelqu'un a dit que je suis paysan parce que je bouffe à six heures du soir mais je n'ai jamais de ma vie mangé de *petrousquin*

Comme tu sais, en latin petra veut dire une pierre, mais *pétrus* n'a assurément rien à faire avec Saint Pierre; l'Eglise de Rome n'est pas fondée sur l'enculement

C'est sans doute un problème pour le philosophe des Ecoles (ou pour le bon docteur Lacan?): est-ce que le *pont arrière* est plus attirant que le Pont d'Avignon? Mais c'est le pons asinorum qui m'attire le plus

Ah non, il y a des bêtises que font les enfants, comme, se magner le *popotin,* qu'on doit oublier; ce n'est pas leur faute, ils ont tant de curiosité, et pourquoi pas, le corps est aussi inexplicable que la vie

Je saute *postère;* toujours la même chose; c'est merdique. Il m'arrive un soupçon honteux: la posterité de Charlemagne aime mieux le cul que le con. Peau de zob, ma défonceuse!

J'ai toujours eu une manque de *pot* avec les fentes, je suis trop monomane, je leur donne des complexes; mais un jour 'y aura une qui verra combien je suis sympa

Tu penses que *prose* veut dire La Rochefoucauld? Polope, ma pisseuse, c'est encore cette histoire d'où sort la merde; mais si c'est de la prose, qu'est-ce que la poésie? Raconte-moi ça!

Ça continue avec *prosinard,* même chose; j'en ai assez, je vais chercher une michette pour me divertir

Et voilà *tafanard;* c'est la même chanson. Ils sont loquaces ces culards, ces shnoques. Ils me font chniquer

Au moins *troussequin* est un mot de quelque substance. Ça vient de trousser, c'est à dire de posséder une femme. C'est pas trop tôt! Elle allait s'endormir

La turbine à chocolat, c'est certainement graphique, ou comme disent les matelots "suivre le chemin de crotte"

"Hello, I'm Marilyn Monroe," j'étais la princesse des *valseurs,* je savais tortiller mes fesses en marchant; toutes les reines des vaches m'ont imitée

Je vais mieux dans la vase, c'est quand j'ai de la chance avec les nanas, quand j'ai du *vase* et je fais zizi-panpan et m'amuse bien.

Sources: François Caradec, *Dictionnaire du français argotique et et populaire* (Paris: Larousse, 1977), and a few phrases from Émile Ajar (pseud. Romain Gary), *La vie devant soi.*

Method: Free association and punning of sounds and sense, some of it interlingual; punning between normal and argotic meanings of words, as in the last verse between "vase"—"rain" and "vase"—"the anus." Some parodic echoes of Flaubert's *Dictionnaire des idées reçues.*

Purpose: A comic commentary on anal eroticism and "la culte des fesses" in France.

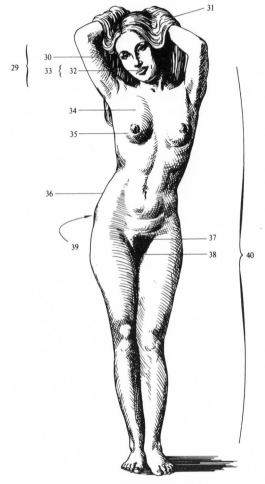

Arrière-train, artiche, baba, baigneur, bavard, brioches, croupion, dargif, derche, dossière, entremichon, faubourg, père Fouettard, gagne-pain, miches, mouilles, noix, panier, pétard, pétoulet, pétrousquin, pétrus, pont arrière, popotin, postère, pot, prose, prosinard, tafanard, troussequin, turbine, valseur, vase.

DON'T SAVE YOUR KISSES

MACLIN BOCOCK

In 1933 when the salaries at the college were cut my father began teasing Mother, saying maybe it was time to sell the silver tray. The tray had been brought from England to Virginia in 1745 by one of her forebears. Mother always gave the same answer. We'd go to the poorhouse first. What we'd done instead was to take in a boarder, Lane Williams—or "paying guest" as Nornie, my grandmother, liked to put it—and we were about to take in another, Blair Reid, coming from Kentucky to work in the college library.

My life improved greatly after Lane came to live with us. He was a candy salesman and covered town and country stores in several adjacent counties, and he was always slipping me a Baby Ruth or Peter Paul Mounds. He kept a small boat on the river and occasionally on Saturday or Sunday, if he wasn't playing golf, he'd take me sailing. And there were evenings when he might say, "Come on, Bits and Pieces," a nickname he gave me, "let's see what's brewing uptown," and we'd jump into his Ford roadster and drive to Brown's or the College Pharmacy for ice cream.

Nornie was right. Even without the mustache Lane would have resembled Clark Gable. In her eyes Lane could do no wrong. He was always kidding her in a gentle way and hardly a week went by that he didn't bring her whatever fruit happened to be in season, raspberries or peaches or winter apples fresh from some farm. I think Nornie imagined him the son she never had and perhaps when he left, it was she who missed him the most.

The afternoon of the evening Miss Reid was to arrive, Lane came back earlier than usual. He was taking a bath, my turn came next, and he was singing a song I found out later was from a new movie playing in Richmond.

> Don't save your kisses
> Just pass them around,
> You'll find my reasoning
> Is logically sound,
> Who's going to know
> You passed them around
> A hundred years from today?

I was in my room and for a moment I had a vision of Lane uptown, standing in front of the post office where the people selling paper poppies on Armistice Day always stood. He was holding out Mother's silver tray piled high with Hershey's chocolate kisses and telling everybody to help themselves. And then I realized it wasn't that kind of kisses he was singing about and I shivered.

When Lane knocked I was looking in the mirror wondering if Miss Reid would like me.

"All yours, Bitsy."

I opened the door. Lane was in his bathrobe, a towel slung over his shoulder and a celluloid soap dish in his hand.

"Remember. People from Kentucky think they're just as good as Virginians, so scrub well. Above all, don't forget the ears."

I stuck out my tongue.

I liked taking a bath after Lane. For one thing he did a good job of cleaning the tub, and I loved the scent of his hair tonic strong in the steamy room.

That evening we were sitting on the side porch waiting for Mattie to call us in to supper. The September heat still held and it was cooler there. A few fireflies drifted around the yard. Our new boarder was arriving on the 8:21 and would be wearing a white eyelet suit and a leghorn hat. My father allowed it was a waste of time Miss Reid writing what she'd have on, as though more than a handful of people ever got off the evening train. After all we weren't Louisville. Nornie claimed she'd yet to meet anyone from Kentucky she hadn't liked and after Mother said she didn't think it very sensible traveling in white, Lane made the remark about Kentucky being famous for its beautiful horses and fast women. It was the first time I had heard the saying.

At supper Lane suggested we all go to the station. Father said that might overwhelm Miss Reid. We'd put our best foot forward and send Lane alone. I could see that Nornie was disappointed but she always leaned over backward not to go against anything my father said. The world was ruled by men and that was the way it should be. She reared my mother accordingly.

I was disappointed, too, but then Lane looked at me.

"At least you must come, Bitsy, and help carry the bags. She's bound to have a dozen."

As it turned out she had only two. In her white eyelet suit and leghorn hat Blair Reid looked as though she had just stepped out on a veranda to greet guests, not taken a long journey with a change and a two-hour stopover. She thanked the conductor who helped her down and turned to greet me. Then she leaned slightly forward toward Lane and again put out her hand.

Blair Reid's appearance—she was beautiful—had the same effect on me as it did on Lane. I managed to get out only one sentence voluntarily, "I hope you had a nice trip." She had and she was happy to be in Virginia again. Again? It was a perfect opening but neither Lane nor I picked up on it. But no matter, for Blair smoothed our silences with a flow of words. She asked questions and made appropriate comments after our replies. Did I have a favorite subject in school? English had been hers, too. She looked forward to living in a small town. She never had before. How wonderful that Lane's job took him to country stores. When she was a child she went with her father on forays looking for antiques in counties around Louisville and they always stopped at some backwoods store to buy pickles. Part of the fun was lifting the top off the barrel and using the long-handled fork to spear the shriveled cucumbers.

That night if anyone had told me Blair's life had been anything but untroubled, I would not have believed it. By the time we had pulled in our driveway, my father halfway down the walk, Mother and Nornie standing on the porch, I knew it was not Miss Craig, my Latin teacher, I wanted to be like but the stranger sitting beside me.

From then on until she left less than three months later, we all danced around Blair, Lane and I swirling the closest. She was twenty-three, two years younger than Lane, and I had just turned fourteen. But she made me feel older talking about things Mother or Father or Nornie would never have mentioned in my presence. Only a few days after she arrived I found myself trying to toss my head the way she sometimes did. I began taking smaller portions of food but lifting my fork without, I knew, the same graceful curve of arm. And I started saving my small allowance to buy Shalimar. As it happened the money was spent on something else because when Blair went back to Kentucky she left her bottle on my bureau with a note saying the perfume was for me.

And Lane? Every other week before Blair arrived he would spend the night in Richmond—he had a cousin there—or get back late, but after Blair came he was always home for supper. And there was breakfast. My mother and father were early risers. Nornie wasn't. Sometimes Lane and I had ours together but more often than not he had gone by the time I was up. But that changed, too. I began listening for the sound of Blair's heels on the steps before I went down and Lane was obviously doing the same thing.

Blair worked crossword puzzles with Nornie and she astounded my father with her knowledge of sports. She fit exactly Mother's idea of a lady. At the end Mother even lied, unheard of for her, trying to protect Blair. As for Mattie, she kept fresh flowers in Blair's room, something she never did for Lane or any of our subsequent boarders. But that was the effect Blair had on everyone she met.

The weeks Blair worked on Saturday she had Wednesday off. On those days I rushed home from school hoping to find her and often she was there waiting for me. Sometimes we would go to the matinée, sometimes walk in what was known as "Tyler's Woods" where paths circled a lake. It was during these walks that Blair told me things about herself that I never revealed not only because I felt they were given in trust, though that may not have been what she intended, but also because they seemed to set us apart.

Blair had been in Virginia earlier as a student at Miss Madeira's. From the first day she hated the school. Once a year St. Alban's choir came to give a concert and once a year the boys at Episcopal High were invited to a tea dance. "Imagine, Bitsy! That was it as far as male company went." Toward the end of the second year she managed to sneak out and meet a young man who had come down from George School. "We didn't do anything wrong." They simply had fun driving around on some of the back roads of northern Virginia.

Blair's dismissal from Miss Madeira's was immediate and final, just what she wanted. But even if they had begged her to return she would not have been able to. Her father would shortly lose everything in the Crash and die of a heart attack. He left some insurance, enough to see her brother through the final year in law school and able to take care of her. But she didn't want that. They had never gotten on. And so she took what seemed to her the best way out. She married. Her husband was from Chicago. But the marriage didn't last. He was jealous beyond belief and would go into a rage if she much as said "good morning" to their sixty-year-old deaf and half-blind postman. After two years she returned to Louisville with a divorce and her maiden name back and a settlement, but no more than was necessary to get a library science degree. She could have come away with a small fortune. Actually she didn't want to accept anything but neither did she want to be dependent on her brother. "Sometimes, Bitsy, you have to swallow your pride."

When Blair told me about her husband we were walking around the lake. The path had narrowed and she was a few steps ahead of me. I was glad because I felt blood rushing to my face. Blair had not only been married, she was a divorced woman! I was sure my parents didn't know this. There was only one divorced person in town, a man, and he was from out of state.

Then Blair murmured, "The worst thing, Bitsy, he abused me physically. He beat me!"

Blair's husband, a white man, did that to her? I knew that Negro men when they got drunk sometimes beat their wives. It had happened to Mattie, but that a white man would do such a thing! How naïve I was. That afternoon when I learned there could be reasons for women to be divorced I felt all the more bound to Blair because I wanted to make up in some way for the suffering that husband had caused her.

Almost from the day Lane came to live with us, I had a crush on him, but it was different from the crushes I had on boys my own age. I would flirt openly with them and write without embarrassment their initials on the front of my notebook, but my feelings toward Lane were secret and involved a life apart. Often before falling asleep I pretended he was holding me in his arms the way they did in the movies, but I never imagined him my husband. What at the time seemed a vast age difference must have prohibited that fantasy. That fact and my worshiping of Blair made impossible any jealousy I might have felt when it became apparent that Lane was in love with her and she in turn was attracted to him. At breakfast if she glanced down to butter a biscuit and I saw Lane looking at her out of the corner of his eye, it was as though he were surreptitiously looking at me. And each time Blair accepted with such grace and pleasure Lane's offer to drop her off at the library, I felt as if I were Lane receiving her favors. So I was not only witness to this drama, I was from time to time playing both roles. I was exhilarated by this secret life, an existence I found far more interesting than my real one.

And so the days slipped by until that Saturday night, or early Sunday morning rather, when I suddenly awoke. Moonlight was spilling through the windows. A few seconds later Blair in a white negligee floated past my room. I thought I was dreaming. But then I heard Lane's door open and close softly. I don't know how long it was before I fell asleep again. I kept seeing them over and over, as though I were there, too, their bodies coming together.

Mother woke me and I had to hurry to get to Sunday school on time. Both Blair's and Lane's doors were still closed when I left.

It was my turn to stay after Sunday school and help put things away and by the time I walked past St. Mark's the service had already begun. There was no one in sight. When I turned onto Spotswood Street I saw it coming, a long black car headed like a bullet toward Richmond. It was one of those moments you never forget, the automobile skimming the street as though about to take to the air, its occupants, the older man sitting up stiffly in the back seat, the younger a white chauffeur in uniform, both staring straight ahead and seeming to hold their breath. Maybe they thought they had to until they cleared the town because if they didn't they might be trapped forever in our backwater community. When they were opposite me—of course it wasn't true but receding time has made it so—the car froze and I saw the older man's jowls hanging, his lips set, the gray felt hat covering what must have been an almost bald head. And perhaps I saw a lap robe across his short, fat legs.

It was not unheard of to see a chauffeured car in town, especially during the autumn or spring when wealthy Northerners were on their way to Florida or on their way home. They would leave the main highway and come the few miles to the college library where there were portraits of several Virginia patriots and a collection of books from the colonial period. The courthouse too was a place of pilgrimage. It had been built after a design of Sir Christopher Wren and because Federal troops had bypassed the town the county records were more or less complete. But when I saw the Georgia license I was sure the man sitting up so straight in the speeding car wasn't an ordinary tourist. In fact I was sure I knew who he was. Friday evening when Blair got in from work I happened to be coming down the stairs and I saw her pick up her mail from the hall table. She ripped open one of the letters. "Mr. Cottingham! I wish he'd leave me alone!" Mr. Cottingham was a wealthy man from Atlanta, old enough to be her father.

I ran a good part of the way home. Mother and Nornie were in church. My father left early that morning to go fishing. I found Mattie upstairs in Nornie's room changing the sheets. If I happened to be around when Mattie was making the beds, I would help.

After their breakfast but before Lane and Blair had driven off together, Blair gave Mattie a sealed envelope with "Mr. Cottingham" written on it and asked her to please give it to the chauffeur when he came to the door. Mattie didn't have to say anything. But knowing Mattie, I am sure she must have a least greeted the man with "good morning."

After we finished Nornie's bed, we went into Blair's room, then Lane's. When we pulled back his covers, in the middle of the bed was a lace handkerchief with the initials "B.R." in blue. Mattie picked it up as though it were the most natural thing in the world to have found there, a piece of lint or a feather escaped from one of the pillows, and without so much as glancing down put it into her apron pocket. She didn't say anything but she looked straight at me and I knew from her eyes she counted on me to keep quiet. That I was now not the only one in the house who knew about Blair and Lane brought me a certain relief but also a certain regret that the knowledge was no longer exclusively mine.

Sunday nights Mattie was off. That evening Mother, Nornie, and

I were cleaning up the kitchen when Blair and Lane got back. Blair came in to see if she could help and reported a wonderful day for sailing, the wind just right. They had a late lunch across the river at a restaurant famous for its seafood. For once she had had enough shrimp. I felt uneasy in Blair's presence and I pleaded homework rather than hang around downstairs. I set my alarm for seven the next morning. I wanted to be out of the house before she and Lane came down.

That day at school my mind wandered more than usual. I kept seeing Blair float past my room or I imagined her in the back of the sailboat, the tiller fastened, her legs stretched out, her head resting in Lane's lap and he looking down at her.

One night some days later I was in my room studying. A few minutes before Blair and Lane left for the nine o'clock movie she knocked on my door. She was planning to sleep late the next morning, her day off, but what about an afternoon journey around the lake? She needed it, librarian stoop and all. I was pleased. I was ready to be alone with her. I knew I would feel better if I told her I had seen Mr. Cottingham. But we never took the walk and what seemed like an appropriate time to bring up Mr. Cottingham never came.

When I got home from school Mother said Blair had decided to go to Richmond to do some shopping. Mother had driven her to the bus station and arranged to pick her up at five. Around four the phone rang. Blair's voice sounded strange but I assumed it was a poor connection. She would be home later, after supper. Had I forgiven her for skipping out? She had something for me and hoped I would like it.

Later Mother and Nornie and Father and Lane were in the living room playing bridge, and when I was on my way downstairs to tell them good night the front doorknob began to rattle. By the time I opened the door Lane had come into the hall. Blair was leaning against the jamb, her hat on crooked and she was wearing only one glove.

"Goddamn door!"

Her tongue seemed to fill her mouth.

"Thanks, Bitsy."

She glanced up at Lane. Her eyes had a glassy look.

"Hi, sweetie. Did you miss me?"

Blair leaned forward and left a smudge of lipstick on Lane's chin. I don't think he could have been more embarrassed had she slapped him. She gave a beautiful smile and handed me a box from Miller and Rhodes. Lane and I watched her move toward the stairs and sink to the steps.

"Oh, God, I'm tired!"

And then she began to cry.

The rest of us thought Blair was drunk but Nornie knew as soon as she saw her eyes that it was drugs. When Nornie was first married she lived in Roanoke next to a doctor whose wife was a "dope fiend." Later Mother asked and my father said there were taxi drivers in Richmond who could have given Blair the information and driven her to get what she wanted.

Mother and I helped Blair to her room. She kept apologizing for being such a bother and saying she could get herself to bed, so we left her. Later Mother went back. She didn't bother about the hat and one glove but she did slip off the shoes and cover her with a quilt Blair had brought from Kentucky.

The present Blair gave me from Miller and Rhodes was a cashmere sweater with pearl buttons. I had the cardigan all during college and was still wearing it when my second son was born, though by then the elbows had been patched several times.

The next morning I pleaded a sore throat, but Mother saw through me and said there was nothing I could do for Blair by skipping school and that she would probably sleep all day. Mother telephoned the library and reported our boarder ill with an upset stomach.

That afternoon when I got home from school I found Mattie in the kitchen. She had just taken some soup and tea to Blair. I put on the sweater and knocked on Blair's door.

"Bitsy, you look beautiful! I knew you would. And it fits perfectly."

Blair was in bed, the tray pushed aside. She had hardly touched the soup. Her eyes had lost the glassy look but she was extremely pale.

"I should have sense enough to stay away from alcohol. Mama had problems with it, too."

And then she wondered if Lane had said anything.

When Lane got in I told him what Blair had asked. He looked

embarrassed but after supper he wanted me to find out if she felt like seeing him for a few minutes.

Did Blair confess the drugs? Describe the depressions when she could not stop crying? The blackness, the longing to escape, even to die? There was a moment of silence before Lane left her room and went down the stairs and out the front door. I wondered if he had kissed her or if they had simply stared helplessly at each other.

Friday morning Blair said she felt fine though she still looked pale and I noticed her hand shake when she lifted the coffee cup. Lane had left early to get to Richmond for a salesmen's meeting. When mother offered to drive her to the library, Blair declined graciously, saying she needed the exercise. We walked together as far as the courthouse where I took the cutoff for school. Later I tried to remember if there was anything she said, any gesture that might have given a hint of what she must have been feeling. In front of the Gardners' house she reached up and pulled down a yellow maple leaf, one of the last on the tree. "Isn't that beautiful, Bitsy?" and then she began to twirl it between her fingers. She must have felt the blackness coming on again and known that before the day was out she would take the bus to Richmond to get what she was desperate to have.

It ended with the brother, unsmiling and tight-lipped, coming from Louisville to take Blair home. The morning they left, Mother let me skip the first three periods of school. At the station when Blair embraced me, she whispered, "Oh, Bitsy," and I thought I heard a faint sob but when she stood back she was smiling like she was sure nothing but happiness lay ahead, and that's the way she looked when Mother snapped the picture of us just as the train pulled in.

That afternoon I slipped into the house by the back door. I wanted to be alone with Mattie for a little while before facing Mother and Nornie and Blair's empty room. When I put my head down on the kitchen table and began to cry, Mattie reached out and touched my shoulder.

"Don't you worry. When she get home she be all right."

During the first weeks after Blair left I wrote her several times before I heard from her. It was a short note. She was in a sanitarium outside Louisville and it was almost as confining as Miss Madeira's! She missed us all terribly, including of course Mattie and her wonderful food. She hoped Lane and I were getting in some good sailing. Sometime later, on a postcard, she told us about her job in a Memphis library. And then for months we heard nothing. Finally Mother wrote the brother, who sent a two-line letter on business stationery signed by a secretary. Blair was back in the sanitarium. In spring of my senior year in high school a large ivory envelope addressed in Blair's hand arrived. The brother had the honor of announcing the marriage of his sister to Mr. Edward Cottingham. An enclosed card gave their address on Peachtree Street in Atlanta.

As for sailing I went only once with Lane after Blair left. That gray November afternoon neither of us spoke of her, but her absence enveloped us like the raw wind blowing up from the bay. In early December Lane put the boat up for the winter and then one evening a few days before Christmas he said he would be leaving in January. He had been transferred to the area just south of Washington. He planned to live in Alexandria and keep his boat on the Potomac. We wondered, but we never found out if he, himself, had asked for the transfer.

It was a sad Christmas with Blair gone and Lane about to leave. But shortly the edge of that sadness would be dulled somewhat by a new boarder, a Mrs. Shaw from Boston who clomped into our lives. She wore corrective shoes and that is exactly what she did. She clomped. After being advised by her doctor to move to a climate where winters were less long and less severe, Mrs. Shaw decided to try a small college town not too far south and after looking at several she chose our community. She inquired at the post office about private homes where one might board and when Mother showed her the two rooms she said she would take them both. She had a son at Harvard who would be coming for spring vacation. Mother protested she could not take money for a bed so little slept in. "Of course you can!" Mother protested no further. One did not argue with Mrs. Shaw. She was a plain woman who made no effort to improve her appearance. She never wore jewelry or make-up. How different from Mother who loved beads and earrings, and Nornie who said she was going to use rouge as long as she could see to put it on. And Mrs. Shaw had a minimum of clothes, two outfits for spring, two for fall. In winter she added a sweater, in summer she removed a jacket. "Why be burdened with more?" I was dazzled by this woman's independence, by the control she seemed to have over her life. She was an active alumna of Radcliffe and she told me at length about the college.

But the arrival of Mrs. Shaw and the windows she opened did not banish Blair and Lane from my mind. I often thought of them. Occasionally Lane sent Nornie some teasing two-line sentence on a postcard and several times a year he telephoned to see how we were. Just before my high school graduation in 1940 a package arrived from a jewelry store in Toronto. It was a silver pin, delicately wrought, a boat, its mast carrying full sail. The card read: "For Bits and Pieces. Congratulations and love, Lane. P.S. I'm now a brilliant member and about the oldest new flier in the R.C.A.F."

When I wrote a thank-you note I told him I had won a scholarship and would be going to Radcliffe in the fall. He answered quickly but with the usual briefness. "So you're headed for the greatest of oceans. Congratulations, but watch those waves!"

Then one night in early November when I was studying for an hour exam, Lane telephoned me from somewhere in Canada. He sounded far away. He had a few days leave and he was thinking of spending them two weekends hence in Boston. Would I be free to show him the sights? He hoped I wasn't becoming so learned we'd have nothing to say to each other. I started to tell him the truth, that he had been right about the waves, but I didn't.

I was elated at the thought of seeing Lane, not because I still had strong feelings for him. I didn't. At that time I was trying to get the attention of my History I section man, the person who would be my first husband. But Lane was a link with Virginia. I'm sure he wanted to come, not to see Boston, but because he too was homesick and with the uncertain future wished to reconnect however briefly with some part of his past.

But on Thursday afternoon of the weekend he was to arrive I found a telegram in my dormitory box. "Complications. Can't come. Please keep the home sails sailing. Love." This could mean only one thing: Lane was being shipped overseas. I spent a sad weekend feeling sorry for him and for myself.

The card he sent at Christmas was addressed to all the family. He was somewhere in southeast England. He had survived two close calls. He'd be much obliged if Mattie would send him some of her fudge. Sweets were hard to come by. There was only one other communication from him, a thank-you note to Mattie, before the announcement in the *Richmond Times Dispatch*. Mother sent me the clipping in the same letter telling about Blair. Blair's suicide in a hotel room in Atlanta had nothing to do, of course, with Lane's death, but in my mind it did because during those brief weeks when Blair was with us, almost from the first moment Lane and I met her at the station, I wanted them to be together and some remnants of that stubborn and impossible wish remained. If not in life, why not in death?

So it was a public war that brought Lane down from the sky into the English Channel, for Blair a private one she had long been destined to lose. The capitulation to Mr. Cottingham must have been a last desperate hope.

For a few days after I received Mother's letter, I kept seeing Blair in the white eyelet suit stretched out in a land-locked grave and Lane's body on the other side of the world drifting along the ocean's dark floor. But those images and the memory of Blair stumbling thick-lipped into the hall, the brother unsmiling come to take her home, have for the most part vanished. What comes back to me again and again is Blair in the white negligee floating down the hall. That and the way Lane looked at her the first time we all went sailing together and the way Blair smiled back. I had never before seen that kind of look between a man and a woman. And even now after all these years, whenever I hear the weather report, the words "from Chesapeake Bay to Cape Hatteras," I see for a moment Lane's boat, full sail, skimming the river's sapphire water. We are sitting, Blair and I, facing Lane, our backs to the bay and he in complete control, his hand on the tiller, and he looks at Blair that way and she smiles back. It is there in my mind, that moment, and safely sealed against the destiny that would encircle Blair and the fate that awaited Lane over other and distant waters.

CHILDREN OF THE MONOSYLLABLE

CLAYTON ESHLEMAN

        I saw a fist
gripping a streaming,
as if beetle-words were flowing into a bottleneck from every-
    whichway,
and that in the slaughterhouse of the fist
they were killed,   and transformed or
            reborn—I could see
the words go in—and what seemed to be their children
        emerge—
they swiveled in like broom straws hungry for the hasp,
        as if they sought to be
bundled,   but as if the broom had not a stick but another
flowering broomhead,
                            the slaughterhouse hasp was the word CUNT,
the beetle-streams, as if emerging from mist, were hard to identify:
        cunnus, yes, cyn, cunta,
parallel to country, kin, kind,
            with shadows of city & cemetery,
cunabula, cunicle, cuniculate, cuneo with its cuneiform kin,
            cunning wedge-words,   vise-signs,
kennings,   beetle-crevices,   kens—or learnings—

Why did they all swarm into this corset that puts
body beetle-words into a round?

"Beetle-words"   because before the corsetgrip
the cunea worked somewhat underground,   they supped from
                Cunti,   or Kunda,
as if attached (somehow) to Her Cuneibrain,   termites?   egg-
carriers?
As if the vulva-lode was slightly under ground-level,
        a cave, or flavoring of stone.
Words once did live across our eyes,
            above and below the Dali razorblade.
And when too many lifted, the sun   roasted our
                            lagoon life?

Language background might have been a termite hill?
A single sound-extent   with a group soul?

So, I've noticed one "hill,"   as if from an airplane,
        the cunae streaming in, as if below meaning,
at what point were thing/earth association words
                    blocked/wedged
                out of themselves, frozen, into
                    their own mimicry?
Or were the cunae slaughtered?   Tonsured, cunta into cunt,
country a cunt-tree pun,   cunicle, cuniculate nearly lost,
blunt   grunt   runt   HUNT
        Monoculture is the reduction/crushing of the millipedal
mania to hit death with a difference

            But why from this round-about phrase must be guessed,
            what in ONE single SYLLABLE'S better expressed;
            That SYLLABLE then I my sentiment call,
            So here's to that WORD, which is ONE WORD for all.

        —G.A. Stevens, *Songs Comic & Satyrical*, 1788.

            And the children? *Diddly-pout, eel-skinner,*
Eve's custom house, mole-catcher, moss-rose, star over the garter,
belly dingle, botany bay, butter boat, cuntkin, cunnie, dumb-squint,
fie-for-shame, fire-lock, flap doodle, oyster-catcher, nonny-nonny,
seed-plot, milking-pail, meat-market, rest-and-be-thankful,

road to a christening, standing room for one, Bluebeard's closet,
catherine wheel, Cupid's anvil, penwiper, mark-of-the-beast,
fumbler's hall, gravy giver, house under the hill, fud,
little spot where uncle's doodle goes, front doormat, snatch-blatch,
rob the ruffian, skin the pizzle, Smock-Alley . . .

       They are attempts to lose her nature from its curse,
but they are not well,   more numerous than their beetle-
   backgrounders
it is as if 30 have shared the same tit.   They spread
into our lives the very air we breathe,
amusing, disgusting, like being in a huge Kroger's Supermarket,
they are flaccid mixtures of the ersatz and the other,
for example, *crinkum-crankum, doodle-sack—*
suppose we placed an honorific monosyllabic offspring before
"sky" or "ocean,"   suppose we tried to indicate that these words are
to be prefaced by monolithic offsprings of the original goddess—
could we do this at all?   Would people catch on?   Would
   they care?
crinkum-crankum sky   [clouds twisting, full of whimsey]
the doodle-sack sky   [wind swollen, bagpipe bleating, god-blast-
   encysted]
Would the great goddess therefore return? Might she invert
   our poisonous world-end anti-ecology?

We would have to as if in flip-flop inversion pass back through
   the bottle-neck,
we'd have to re-experience, in another conscious first-time,
what the language-mind suffered,   we'd have to run the *whim-wham*
sperm-sucker fie-for-shame film backwards,   as we ourselves
assimilated the peril of the reduction of woman,
   her identity crunched into a monosyllable

   CUNT as termite-queen
   laying 50,000 associations per day in male mind,
nether eye-brows, itching Jennies, roasting jacks,
seeking to escape into fulfilling linguistic cores?

Might we adopt these orphans?   Might we even nurse them?

Yes, we might croon: under your flossy levers
I hear the RA, the OM, the KA
     lingering gas,   and GOD   that poor rotten cork
for a bottle that wanted only to be sipped and sipped—

little *mark-of-the-beast,* little *gutter,*
     you bear the stink of a degradation
you are hardly responsible for.
But should *gutter* then respond: I am happy to be
    a receptacle for dead leaves, rain, dead pigeons,
An inferior form of Kunta's cunabula?
    No, I said, you are cunabula form!
True—I'm not life-emitting.   I'm a drainpipe a deathpope,
and the men who have used me, who have passed out of
barbershop and prison me and my brothers,
they are the slaughterhouse tongues.

     So each word *does* have a personality!
A background, a heaven and a hell, and a future.
Each word, a "mighty limb of Albion,"
a forfeit, an excuse, a Mumonkon, a dragon-tongue on
    the hinge of axial powers.
Gutter Cunabula convinced me.   Each word, or word-resizing,
clitorized? a core, Every word my equal,
    every word's amphibian sound-tail,
suckers what I cannot quite discern, that is, it sinks
a nippled tentacle into the termite flow, as the word mites
bless, as they bang and bank off, as they scurry
egg-laden, in absolute midden to what I shall not be
    delivered to see,
but I can hear their vacuum nourishing the rust of a passing
  train,
     a halo-ford, the poet can dunce into,
shroud and nave of the sordid cleat of tongue
angling, as if my tongue were an angel flue, lifting
    whatever,
the grub of this desk, serendipity of the frontis-claw,
the eyes of dyked intrepidity at rest

TWO AMERICANS

H. D.

1

He said, "Daniel is a lovely fellow." Their faces remained faces yet for all that, those faces had turned now forever into static symbols, they were mask on contrasting mask, the one white, the other as it happened, black. The two Americans faced each other in a crowded little living room, overlooking the Savoy Grammont.

Saul Howard said, "Daniel is a lovely fellow," and in that moment Raymonde Ransome felt click into place *her* place, saw established in time, for all time, *his* place. It was hardly a question of the personal thing, there was no personal equation. That had been solved for her some time since, at the completion of that very so-Great War; for him, he had been always at war. They met in a field of honour, herself entirely defeated, himself yet to be acclaimed for some kingship the world is not ready to recognize. He was no black Christ. He was an earlier, less complicated symbol. He was the Dionysus as Nietzsche so valiantly struggled to define him; possibly she stood vaguely for counter balancing Nietzschean Apollo, though where he was complete, she was strikingly deficient. She was deficient, even, you might say, crippled in some psychic song-wing; his song flowed toward all the world, effortless, full of benign power, without intellectual gap or cross-purpose of hypercritical consciousness to blight it. There was no swerving from the beginning, the root, the entire deep in-rooted power of his gigantic Being. He was really no person at all. Seated opposite him, on the

58

orange-lacquered low wooden seat that Gareth had had specially designed for just that fire-side corner, Raymonde knew that. She let her own personality harden, "fix" as it were; now she would be this forever. For her, the "voice" was speaking. It spoke to the world, every gramophone window displayed Saul Howard's records. The voice spoke on everybody's wireless. Howard himself was, in fact, on his way back to London, stopping off here from his concert in Vienna. The voice that spoke on everybody's wireless, spoke now to her intrinsically. It said, "Daniel is a lovely fellow."

2

There had never been any doubt in her mind of Daniel. He was a cup to be protected, the crystal that he was, was brittle, people drew away from Daniel, shocked by some vibration that they could not assimilate. The vibration of Daniel Kinoull was violet-ray for the majority. There had never been any doubt in the mind of Raymonde Ransome about Daniel. Only, it was shattering enough in all consciousness, to have that consciousness forever alone to cope with. Not that people didn't recognize the finesse, the sleek greyhound sort of fibre of him. That wasn't it exactly. There was something of him that she wore alone, like a steel pin in her side. She felt herself stiffen, she felt herself harden as she felt at just that moment, that somehow, some way that pin had been pulled out. It was no more there. She had grown so used to this thing that she realized it now in its entirety, only as it had gone. As the voice lowered to note of intimacy, she saw the thing was out. She wouldn't wear Daniel Kinoull anymore like a martyr's jacket. She wouldn't have the sort of hair shirt now anymore to efface the somewhat weather-worn marble that she was. Weather-worn marble, Raymonde Ransome, faced Saul Howard, seared bronze.

Complete by just that miracle, she felt her face that in "all time," was so static, just in "this time," slipping. Her face slipped, a distorted superimposition on a placid mask of marble. The present-day features struggled to readjust, to become one again with the eternal symbol. They almost made it, but she felt the quivering of muscles about her eyes betray her; she caught in her underlip, managed the thing finally. The words she spoke were exactly and appositely the thing his were not, the voice was pitched too high, nerve-strained, the words were ill-defined, just somehow,

"Daniel made all the difference . . . it was all difficult . . . I mean, he brought back my faith." As the voices of the others broke across their own steady murmur and Gareth, first out of the dining room, said, between the two groups, "the coffee's in here," Raymonde got the thing right. Her face was just the quite ordinary face she used for ordinary purposes; a bath sponge, a bath mat, a dish of boiled potatoes would be as useful, as aesthetically efficient. Nevertheless, she congratulated herself on the fact that it *was* efficient, as Paula Howard entered.

3

She quickly tightened that mask, screwed, as it were, the flexible edges tighter as they came. Her face turned toward them, she revolved, in just that sort of basic sort of cycle that he had shown her was his way of turning when he said (in Terence Deal's play) "I ain't no longer any poor white's chattel." So he had worked out a sort of circular stage gesture that, as he had demonstrated it, had shown her all time, all slaves, all whites, all hunted and war-ridden creatures. His least movement was so gracious, he didn't have to think things out. Nevertheless, with an astonishing analytical power, he did think. That was the odd thing about Saul Howard, he did think. He had a mind, a steadfast sort of burning, a thing that glowed like a whole red sunset or like a coal mine, it was steady, a steady sort of warmth and heat, yet all the time intellectual; he thought not as a man thinks. Paula Howard, his wife, thought more as white folks, consistently, being more than half white. Her voice was her almost chief attraction, almost one forgot, as she spoke, the words that so often belied the thing she spoke of. Her notes were drawn out, tropic bird-note from a throat across which the double row of pearls brought out her almost tea-rose colour. Her face, if she would let it be, was tea roses, glowing amber beside his dark, steady burning. The face of Paula Howard was beautiful, her voice held exquisite inflection. All the same, wheeling now to face her, with, she realized, a very fair imitation of Saul's hunted Negro revolution of Terence Deal's play, Raymonde felt that the mask, fitted under her casual flung-forward hair, was tightening. She felt the very process of the tightening, an inflexible subconscious thing, while all the time she thought, "why really she is right. We owe her everything. He is lazy. I don't believe Saul Howard would have troubled to have stopped off here, if it hadn't been for Paula. I don't even believe he would in the least be where he is, acclaimed by everybody on everybody's wireless and in all the gramophone shops, if it weren't for Paula."

Raymonde knew, by that very swiftness of her induction, that already she was putting up barrier of "being fair" to Paula, because something deeper than this inductive wisdom already wanted to betray her. Intellectually, she was quite fair, but something deeper than her reason was somehow boiling over. She realized how near it was to the boiling point, therefore she could yet check it. She wouldn't however let that holy spark die out. She would shelter it. She would do everything in her power to see they had a good time, to see that they took Daniel's work to heart, to see that everything went nicely. She would see to this, to this, play pack mule for Paula even. Something already warned her. She said, moving aside to let the others crowd on and near Saul, "Sit down here, Paula."

They all wanted to crowd round Saul. It was an instinct really. They were so many somewhat rain-drenched butterflies, opening wings in his presence. It seemed ironical that Paula who didn't get this, who wasn't like them, who was the one of the whole crowd who didn't get his authentic quality, should be the one to vamp it. She must sit directly opposite Saul, must watch each twitch of muscle, must tabulate each little gesture, must explain to Daniel, "But how funny, you English people never know Saul is joking." Daniel, set inflexible and upright, showed, by not so much of a quiver of an eyelash, that this remark betrayed her. He simply negated Paula, yet all the time in his exquisite way, he played up to her. He flung his very direct and charmingly directed little compliments, the just right moment for offering her a cigarette, his way of holding the match for her; he had already admired her pearls, said how much he wanted to film her. He did want to film her. Raymonde drew right out, managed to sit in the room, yet almost out of the room, crouched by the side wall with Gareth. They had all agreed, on various occasions, that the place was too small.

4

The place which theoretically now should have been dwarfed out of any recognition, opened up like a rose-peony. It didn't matter what the man said and there was no use clutching at him. One couldn't ask him to sing; if only someone would make him keep on talking. Daniel turned his entire attention to concentrate on Paula. No doubt he was studying her, he would do his utmost with her. To Daniel, the woman opposite was just this or that effect of light and shadow, no doubt he was wondering what sort of make-up would do best. He would see and want to stress just that light gold wash of tea-rose colour, a thing the film couldn't yet catch. He would then concentrate on her turn of chin and the way her blue-black hair waved like a black wing over one cheek. The other cheek was naked, the asymmetry of her hair was striking and Paris and chic. Paula was Paris, was striking, yet, all the time, she made it very clear that she was not to be confounded with that tribe who had given jazz to Europe. She had attained something for which something had been sacrificed. For the very valour of her achievement, someone should warn her just what it was she left out. Yet who was there now to warn her and what really had she lost? The tragedy of Paula was that just Paula as herself would be so far more interesting than most of their white friends. The tragedy was that she showed up horribly her deficiencies beside Saul.

But who, Raymonde asked herself, didn't?

5

Bennie Matthews looked ridiculous. He loved Saul too much. It didn't do to love an earthquake or a mountain with just that human sort of poodle-dog affection. Affection itself was perhaps too human and too pliable an emotion for any of them. You couldn't let yourself go, didn't dare just love him. For where would that lead? Raymonde, with one arm schoolgirlishly about Gareth's shoulder, asked herself that. Gareth was small, clad in her own perfection. Gareth was perhaps the one best fitted to approach Saul. She had talked to him of the desert, Bedouins, various native African voodoos, the plains and hollows of the lower valleys of the Nile. Gareth, as a child, had spent all her winters out there. Gareth was almost, in that, more deeply affiliated with Saul than any of them. She had propounded pedantic little queries that had made the great mouth widen in that smile of blessing. Looking down at Gareth as a giant on some indomitable little pixy, Saul Howard had let shine the glow of that smile. Well, perfectly Raymonde knew, the fields that year would harvest. She hadn't read her *Golden*

Bough for nothing. She knew perfectly, this year, the heavy grain would bend over the slender wheat stalks; there was that burden in his blessing. She knew all that, she felt Gareth had more than her share of it. She felt Gareth, in her odd little way, had opened perhaps as none had. Bennie Matthews was too restive, too haunted, too really upset. Daniel was by a shade of a fraction of emotion too detached. Raymonde had her little job of scribe and priestess, watching outside. Perhaps Gareth, the best, responded.

But that was the way with Gareth. Having flung out her little challenge this afternoon, her precise little morsel of authentic first-hand knowledge of that special Bantu tribe who "sing" the hippo-potamus out of the river, she let slide back. She let the door shut, she looked out of her own window. But with her arm schoolgirlishly flung about Gareth's shoulder, Raymonde knew that she and Gareth looked out of the same window.

6

Their own apartment was too small, so they usually put their guests downstairs. They could always get those rooms in the wing of the Gräfin Neuhault's place, the old lady was economizing and anyhow was now in Egypt. Bennie had what was presumably the ex-Gräf's smoking room, done up with sleeping couch and prewar hunting trophies; the two Howards had the suite facing the Lake. Paula and Saul went downstairs early. That was part of Paula's tact. Raymonde was the only one who could exactly realize, how exactly and precisely Paula was doing the right thing and doing it better than it could possibly have been done by any mere white. There was a sort of ironical and altogether devastating pleasure to be got out of watching Paula's not inconsiderable tactics. Raymonde, however, resented a little the fact that she was the only one of their little group precisely qualified to gauge the whole of Paula's quality.

Bennie appreciated all this but didn't exactly "get" it. He was too true-to-type, young Londoner, journalist, essayist, general utility man to one of the superior Quarterlies. Bennie had his London at his fingertips. In fact, they would never have got to know Howard, in just that incredible manner, if it hadn't been for Bennie.

Bennie drew a deep breath. He sidled over toward the vermillion lacquered settle that Gareth had had designed by the little shop in Berlin. Bennie said, "What is it about Paula?" Each of them in her, or his, several manners would always come back to Paula. The miracle remained unexplained, the Sphinx riddle had no answer. Paula had Saul. Why? How had it happened? Bennie told them. "She said the four most likely young bucks of Harlem wanted her. She said, then I saw Saul Howard strolling along Broadway with a Phi Kappi Nu key and a gold football trophy dangling from his watch chain, and I said *now that's my man!*" Raymonde interpreted, "It wasn't Broadway and it wasn't Phi Kappi Nu and Paula would never have said 'now that's my man.'" Bennie said, "Don't swank, Raymonde, just because" (he was being funny) "you and Saul and Paula are Americans."

Raymonde must appeal to Bennie. There seemed, at the moment, no one left to go to. Wasn't it Bennie who had asked them all, just last spring in London, if they would want to meet Howard? Saul Howard? The name was a name in everyone's gramophone box, on every sort of wireless. "But Bennie . . . is he actually a person?" Words had streamed out of corners, words had joined words and once actually at a London music hall, Saul Howard had interpolated one of his incredible spirituals in the middle of a shocking musical comedy. But even that distant far-removed creature had looked somewhat of a shadow. Saul Howard on that particular stage, had come up almost Paula colour, the footlights bleached him, he looked then and from the distance of the dress circle, a light mulatto, as Gareth put it, "one of those Harvard niggers who talk English."

They had dismissed Saul Howard as a highbrow sort of over-educated Negro, who was descending, out of some superior idea of fashionable race loyalty, to singing spirituals of the moment. Saul Howard interpolated oddly into that London music hall, was oddly not that. His heart that afternoon had not been in the thing that he did. Nevertheless, across that packed house, there was a ripple of delicate blue grass, there was a flight of cardinal butterflies. Oddly and for almost the first time, in her tragically rooted London war-consciousness, Raymonde Ransome felt that America was her home.

7

Gareth went to see Bennie to his room. Daniel said, "I can see the man had an incredible fascination for you." Raymonde said, "Fascination?" She did not know what he meant. She shoved the tray to one side, regretted that someone had put a glass down on the bare table, brushed the circle out with her handkerchief. "I wish people wouldn't put tumblers on this table." Daniel said, "I can see that. I can see how you reach out to him." Raymonde jerked back into consciousness of Saul Howard. "O . . ." she tried to yoke Saul up to the thing Daniel hadn't got right. "No . . ." "Yes, I can see it. I don't mind, it's all right. Of course, you ought to see more people. You are so terribly in-grown, cut off." She couldn't fasten the thing together. She couldn't find words in which to explain to Daniel. After all, she had never talked about America except to execrate its horrors as they all did. "Saul?" The man's name was Saul. She realised that his name was that. But "Saul" as Daniel said it and the thing that she knew, didn't in the least tally. There were no words, only images. The image of the moment was a bleeding-heart bush and a minute crocodile in a cigar box that someone had sent her grandfather from Florida.

Home? Raymonde Ransome had found that; her spiritual home was Gareth, was Daniel. Both with burning grey eyes that matched her own eyes burning, they were more "related" to her than anyone ever had been. They were related to her as Katherine had been related. But Katherine, in America, even then had been far removed from the thing that now held. Katherine would understand this . . . but Katherine had let go things through being "European." You can be more European than Europe in America . . . does the converse too hold? Can you be more American than America in Europe?

"Why no—" she let the ring go. It didn't matter who had put the glass there. "No. It's a problem, you wouldn't understand it." She was looking across a room, across a tray of assorted liqueur glasses and whiskey and soda tumblers. She was facing Daniel. "No, it's altogether this way. You see," she was surprised herself to hear what she said, "he's removed a silver thorn out of my side, called Daniel."

8

She moved across the room, demolished it as she moved. She swerved with that basic circular movement, that sort of hieratic turn that Saul had shown her. Is it true that every movement of an arm, a leg, the swerve forward of a torso, the lilt of a head thrown backward, has power? Is it true that movement of the human body throws out, as it were, a sort of charted series of tabulated vibrations, so that just that circular turn, Greek bronze on rotating pedestal, did this thing? Raymonde, self-conscious, lost self; she revolved again; "This is the way he said he moved when the imaginary host of whites rises, off stage, in Deal's play." She made the circular gesture, the room was obviously too small. Herself, seemed to have grown to some disproportion, seemed to stand equal to him. If she could let go things fantastically in-grown, she might yet be Saul Howard's equal. She said, "We have lost something. I mean everyone but . . . you."

She had argued this point so frequently with Daniel. There didn't seem much use now beginning. He wouldn't, or he possibly couldn't, see what he was. Perhaps if she somehow managed to show him the thing about him, to conjure up some definitive Dodonian forest and say, "This is the thing you are *not*, this is Saul Howard," then she could, by the same logic, show him a whittled piece of marble, the thing that might stand at the entrance to just such magic woodland. She might be able to demonstrate marble, Apollo, contrast shadow and leaf-grove, Bacchus. This she might conceivably do, if without deterrent, she herself ran on those rails. She must see both, be, in a way, both and yet she must commit herself to neither. She said, "It's stuffy in here, too crowded with their auras. Come out (there must be a moon or something) on my balcony."

He would follow her across a room that might or might not be a sort of cella. She might see in the dark-blue shadow (the far wall of curtains) a small winged Psyche with a marble mouth that pouted somewhat forward like the early Michelangelo *Eros* of the South Kensington in London. She might see image from Crete transposed to a mouldy basement in a dissociated sort of lost Museum somewhere, or she might, with some reversion to the peculiar consciousness that she had, call right out, "Come here" to this or this manifestation of divinity, and just that image would stand there against those curtains, not marble but flesh and fire, blood and brawn. She had a peculiar sort of feeling of walking right out of the crowded little living room, where they had smoked too much over cognacs and coffee, and to be standing on the thin edge of something, just about to be able to make everything come true. She could, she was certain, disestablish at any rate for herself, a certain sort of monster, the thing that said "Thou shalt kill" for instance. "Thou shalt kill" reversed commandments for her. She had taken that ever-so-great War too seriously. She recalled "Thou shalt kill" far, far too personally; it had become for her an actual blood-Minotaur or a sort of blood lust incarnate. But the woods, her peculiar forest had perhaps, for that very reason, become personified . . . she had to clutch hold of the corner of her low-set bookshelf to show herself where she was. She said, "Daniel, if we ever get this thing right, everything will come right."

She didn't know exactly what she wanted to get right but Daniel would know. If she could keep Daniel true to the thing called Daniel (that he didn't know was there) she would be able to decipher . . . messages. Exactly now, there was exact message; it faced her. Exact message seemed to be written with a sort of lightning-crayon across the blue-black depth of the Savoy Alps beyond her. Standing now with the blue-curtained long French window flung wide open, Raymonde said to Daniel, "You see everywhere . . . it's written." It might not be written everywhere but it was written there assuredly; a white line made cryptic scrawl exactly opposite. True, the phosphorescent tenuous line, against luminous blue-black, was the snow-edge of the Grammont against Alpine sky. Still, even with the footlights, so to speak, from the area beneath her, just the least discountenancing vision, it seemed to Raymonde that the mountain had said something. She seemed again to be standing on the thin edge of something, just about to be able to make everything come true.

9

Daniel said, "Someone's having a bath, I think in number 14." Raymonde peered down the almost New York area. Downstairs, about four flights down, there was a window flung wide open and the sound of water running. Someone shut the window, as they watched, like a clever bit of cinema "montage," and then from above (more "montage") the girl who always left her skis on the roof for someone else to fetch in, called angrily down the area, "Ma-aa-a-daline." Raymonde said, "Shall I get Louise to let that girl in, with our roofkey?" Daniel said, "No, damn her . . . she's always getting locked out," and they peered down the area again like two people leaning over a ship rail, avid with the small curiosities that people have on shipboard. The area dropped, elongated parallelogram, picked out with little windows. "It's a pity," Raymonde went on, "Saul and Paula are on the side facing the lake. It would be so funny to watch their lights go on, go out." Daniel said, "For an intelligent woman, you have the curiosity of a skiv." Raymonde said, "Yes, I rather flatter myself I have. The Barton twins stayed over time this Easter." Daniel said, "I met the colonel going to play golf." "Golf," said Raymonde, "yes . . . we're awfully incarnated here, in our small way." Daniel said, "Incarnated? Aren't we everywhere?" Raymonde laughed, "No . . . no . . . no, no, no . . . not always." She clung fast to the iron rail; it was cold to her hands. She slid her palm along the rail; warm that or let that warm her. She clung to particularization, the Barton twins, the girl on the roof whom someone else had let in, the lights that now for the most part were put out. "These area windows are people's servants' rooms and their bathrooms. I'm glad we have this small flat, under the roof, we're out of all that." This one flat, miniature of the more pretentious ones, was fitted, as it happened, against the mountain where their garden, really on a level with the long, railed-in house roof, seemed to be sunken in, as from the road above it. So all mental states, Raymonde often thought, were adequately to be measured, exactly shelved here. She stood on the Swiss side, as it happened, and looked across an almost New York drop, down a ten-story area, then up to the Grammont opposite.

They were Swiss, they were French, with just that narrow upper arm of Lake Léman to measure them off. States, people, nations—it was all a matter of a slice of water or a muddy river or the shattered edge of a blood-spattered precipice, to go by.

"Mohammed and the mountain," said Raymonde, facing, as it happened the ridge of the French Grammont, "did or didn't it come to him? It's come to me anyway. I mean," she said, "America."

OVERHANG

Extracts

PHILIPPE DENIS

Translated by Cid Corman

> *The first step*
> *awakens the path.*

❀

To be clear!   but as
a corolla constantly surprised   which discovers
blue   with its storm-blue
                              To be burst-clear!

❀

Drawn up. Purple. To glove what wind? The
                digitalis

Like friendly, the trembling proffered—in
          this flower . . .

(a day's ember
             —rag hearth

✿

I've counted again   to subtract myself from
                         this gray beardless
sum.

✿

Silence interrupts, punctuates   , casts out
beyond, in the time when we had never dreamt
that speaking could precisely interrupt
silence.

✿

Child   —your angel crutches.

✿

To be there   then to have been there
—the porousness of a moment.

✿

I pass   only to obey this voice—
lodged
        in the excited mouth of night.

✿

Rest   such as the scything allows to
the time of a whetting.

✿

Mouthful of earth   you have the taste
of a word,
                    of a word containing horizon

✿

Everything's there   as
if always   everything had been there
at this starting point   hard to see.

                              ✿

Struck dumb, on this way, by the thunderbolt—
have I now the severity of a cloud . . .

✿

Flowers—to the point of naming   then crumpling.

✿

I listen to the earth   , that future
beating of wings which reascend from the
lowest point.

✿

Overhang   word containing   the word that
breaks

            the wing.

✿

The key shines   —it's the darkness of
                    tomorrow.

OLD MAN FINDS WHAT WAS LOST

JAMES B. HALL

That time was in Ohio long ago when people lived on farms and
did the work themselves but had electric lights inside the rooms
and a radio to get the News and tractors and many well-known
animals such as cows. Also many dogs in the farmyard all barking
and running around in circles.

Farmer and Old Woman lived and worked on just such a farm;
for many a year it was corn, hogs, wheat, and soybeans or maybe
clover. Once they had children about the house, but not anymore
as three daughters, each in turn, went off to live a better life in
Cincinnati.

One August about midnight Farmer stood on his front porch and
looked out across his ninety-two acres of corn and heard the corn
growing, making springy little noises in the dark, clear back to his
woods. Farmer looked once at the sky and then he locked all out-
side doors, but did not go very fast upstairs to where their bed was.

First, as was customary, Farmer turned off the electric light and
then took off all his clothes and then laid hisself down beside Old
Woman.

—Hotter, Farmer said, than a half-fixed fox in a forest fire.

Even when he didn't know it, Old Woman understood every-
thing about Farmer; therefore, his remark told Old Woman what
was on Farmer's mind—maybe.

As that thought was some real change in things, Old Woman
decided to find out the lay of the land.

Old Woman half-rolled over to Farmer's side and she placed her leg almost on top of his leg. Old Woman felt she had the rights of it because Farmer hisself first mentioned fox.

Very softly Old Woman said into the pillow beside Farmer's ear, "Hooo?"

In times past when Farmer was young or had just returned from the stockyards with money or of an afternoon walked through his barns to view breeding stock or if the corn was well along, then he nearit always said,

—Hooo, yourself . . . ? and then in various ways the job got done, and that was that.

In the past there had been some real Hoooing around. But lately not much, which is what is being said.

As was natural, Old Woman understood Farmer was getting on in years. Moreover, the three girls were no longer about the house, taxes were up some, the neighbors talked drought, drought, and of recent date a blood virus taken down two shoats per week, all of which signified losses for everybody.

Well, this very day, Old Woman, herself, had done no work—except a little fancy tatting. She skipped the News and went direct upstairs full well knowing Farmer was soon to follow as he did not much like to be alone in the rooms of their house. Old Woman had something on *her* mind.

—I pass, Farmer said, and for the first time in his life felt bad to renege—the corn being so well along. To renege made him feel unnaturally old. Farmer had well-noted Old Woman tatting fast all afternoon, so knowed he was in for it.

Old Woman did not say anything at once for she understood his remark might be natural for a man of his years, though otherwise healthy and of good appetite.

Nevertheless, three months of I Pass was a considerable time. So Old Woman retch over and with her hand slid down the nice black hair of Farmer's belly. With her hand sometimes, as in play, she would find it and then take aholt of his business.

This time no business. Nothing—so to speak—for Old Woman to take aholt of.

—That's why I passed, Farmer said, and he was put out to let her know. Seems I lost it. Lost . . . my business.

Again Old Woman said nothing. But since she knew all of that territory very well, had looked it over many a time in broad daylight, she just very gentle, gentle searched around. Just looking for herself with her woman hand.

Old Woman was also some surprised. As Farmer claimed, there was not much; in fact, nothing in the whole territory.

Then Old Woman whispered very kindly in his ear, "Well, let's just see about this," and before Farmer could say I, Yes, No nor Flour, why out of their bed she sprang and turned on the electric light and—bang—she pulled back their coverlet.

And that was that.

For Old Woman to see him like that was always a sight: good legs and arms, and those shoulders, and his face maybe a little creased from the work and the sun as though afloat on the clean sheets, and ifn he opened those eyes, they was blue as an ocean.

Very closely, she inspected the whole territory, a thing which even under the circumstances gave some trifle of pleasure. Then she turned out the light, got back in bed, and caused herself to lie down next to Farmer. Hooo, she said, it's some little thing. Besides Hog Futures are steady, the girls are happy in Cincinnati, and your corn is well along. Tomorrow I'll kill us a chicken, largely for the dumplins.

In his mind, Farmer saw what she said in clear pictures. There was much to be thankful for, so after the chicken wouldn't they just rock on the porch and listen to the corn grow?

Old Woman went to sleep and then Farmer went to sleep—called it a day.

Well, no change in the Hooing, but Old Woman saw Farmer look everywhere: looked in the little tool box under the seat of the wheat binder; among sacks of clover seed because of the sweet, attracting smell; looked under the Leghorn hen because of her steady warmth, but nowhere around the place was his business to be found.

Not found, not mentioned, was Old Woman's thought and besides, twixt her and the gate post, she understood nothing was really lost; gradually it had become smaller and smaller, and now it was back where it came from. So at this moment it was at hand, in Farmer's belly. So to Old Woman it boilt down to this: salt the cow to get the calf, for she knew of old that it was never out never up.

In her ways, Old Woman was very smart, so the morning after

Labor Day, as was her plan all along, she lay abed. No reason stated.

Come noon and Farmer went to the bedroom to see about it, there being no dinner cooked.

Still Old Woman faced the wall: taken her bed.

Four days passed and no meals forthcoming, so towards noon Farmer was back again to the bedroom and in effect said, We ought to Doctor. We ought to Doctor some.

"No Doctoring," Old Woman said very bravely. "It's too much money." Which was a point.

Four more days passed, and no change. Mostly to get things organized, and also because Old Woman could be stubborn as the off-mule in a sorghum mill, in effect Farmer said, You will have it, so I'll fetch the Bailey girl from town. She can look to your needs and cook some, and how much all-found a week oughten I offer her mother?

"Whatever is right," Old Woman said, and faced the wall.

So next day, from town, up pulls Farmer in his automobile and he parks it in the center of the barnyard.

Farmer gets out. He walks him around the radiator, and he open *her* door. Out steps this Bailey girl: all found, and wearing a starched, all-white uniform borrowed of her mother (also betimes a practical nurse).

Then all Billy-bedamned braked loose in that barnyard: dogs barking and running in circles; the yellow she-cat and half her litter a-streaked for the crib; Jim-the-Crow calling *Hey-Petey, Hey-Petey* from the grape arbor; the two mules poked their heads out the hogpen winders.

That Bailey girl were a lot better framed than most. Also a red-head. Also in the wind of the ruckus, holting down her dress hem with one hand, that Bailey girl's all-white uniform roilt up everything.

All of which signified not much in the bedroom, in private, when Old Woman laid out the work expected:

"Some light housekeeping," Old Woman said, and sat up real sprite on the edge of her bed. "But don't feed too heavy."

The Bailey girl took Old Woman's meaning: easy on the meat.

"And this next is betwixt just the two of us: though active, Farmer has got two failings. One, the left ear is not quite deef as a fence post. Second, his sight. Things close at hand he can not see too good—like handtools, or a knife and fork. Naturally, Farmer has his pride so he never lets on. Even to me.

"That's why," Old Woman continued, "Farmer is your real patient, but pretend it is me. Stay plenty outside with him, and from time-to-time I'll get my own tea water."

The Bailey girl took Old Woman's meaning: speak up to the left ear; help find little things at hand; keep a shut mouth, especially to Farmer.

"All correct," said Old Woman, and began to straighten up her bed.

Meanwhile Farmer was gone to the barn to see why two mules poked their heads out of two winders of a brood sow's pen.

Inside bright and early for two weeks it was a redhead and a white uniform in the kitchen. It was "Here's you aigs—no bacon, it's too dear"; it was "Here's your coffee and your knife," and she took Farmer's hand and gentle found him his fork.

"Also," says the Bailey girl, and because Farmer flinched some she knew his hearing was some better, so she whispered real close, "And here's your napkun."

—Yes sir, Farmer said, and he thought, Napkun for breakfast?

For two weeks outside it was the Bailey girl helping Farmer, her white uniform now normal, the stock not roilt up. Farmer was looking for something, like a blind dog in a meat house. Naturally, Farmer couldn't exactly describe it to a stranger, so the Bailey girl did her best, fetched him bolts, a lynch pin, a staple puller, a clevis, and held them close to Farmer's nose and said, "Is this it?"

Course it never was.

Gradual, however, Farmer gave it up, and only slicked down some harness, greased all wagon axles, and cleaned some clover seed. But the Bailey girl was there, *handing* him every little thing, close, and sometimes more so.

Then Old Woman heard Farmer sing "Tenting Tonight" in the privy, and his laid-by corn never looked better. From her upstairs winder, Old Woman saw a white uniform always by Farmer's side. Well she noted Farmer was getting lively, and more so, which is what is being said.

So: the Bailey girl is in the corncrib. To get something dropped, she laid herself down and she rotched between some sacks of clover seed, stretch out crosswise in her white uniform on the sacks.

Suddenly Farmer went outside to relieve hisself. And, well, there it was. Back in the same territory: he found his business.

Farmer came running back to the crib—to tell someone the news. He saw the Bailey girl laid out on the clover sacks and Farmer just couldn't help hisself. He pinched her. Right there. On the uniform.

The Bailey girl come up off the clover sacks like a she-cat at weaning. She cuffed Farmer. On his good ear.

"If I want my ass pinched," she yelled, "I'll get it done in town and I quit."

So the Bailey girl packed her jockey box and Old Woman paid her off and Farmer drove her back to town no words spoke.

Back home Old Woman was hard at it: smoke in the kitchen, and a nice fryer in the pan.

"Good riddance," Old Woman said without hard feelings. "Hired help is never the same and she wasn't feeding you anyways near enough meats. And I knew it."

Old Woman began to hum a song over the stove and everything was organized and back to normal.

That night in their bed, right away, Farmer said "Hooo . . ." and Old Woman said "Why Hooo, your self—."

And the job got done. And for some time there was plenty of Hoooing on the old home place in one way and another.

Though never so much as mentioning the Bailey girl again, the Old Woman thought this: it helped Farmer over a little drought and she, herself, got some much needed bedrest. So the expense was just about fifty-fifty, and it might be called Doctoring. Besides, they had never talked Florida vacation or anything like that.

What is general knowledge, howsomeever, is this: a few years later, whilst weeding an iris bed, Old Woman just died. Soon thereafter Farmer died of a broken heart because he couldn't stand being alone in the rooms of their house.

Also general knowledge: the three daughters came home and naturally put the land, the stock, and all machinery to public auction. Jim-the-Crow went back to the woods; bids on all livestock was stronger than expected.

The daughters settled their three shares with no hard feelings and went their separate ways back to the City.

And that is how Farmer found what was temporary lost.

MNEMOGASOLINE

ANDREI CODRESCU

Under the tropical moon
the peaceful hooker
discoursed on the Gestalt God
with a cat on her shoulder
slowing the motorists down.
She was without fear
as the small Honda went past
bound for the warfront against auto-amnesia
being waged on the old narrative line of defense.
The Honda stopped and a technical
designer at Disney Studios,
who that very day
had been observed doodling on the job
a thing unrelated to Mickey,
and accused of spying,
got out and advanced toward her.
Rather than apologizing, I quit,
he to her explained.
Go to sleep,
said the peaceful hooker.
She wore white stretch pants
& a red sweatshirt inscribed OPIUM
& she took his hand and laid him
on the steps at Sproul Plaza in Berkeley.

He woke up surrounded by a forest of sleeping bags.
A protest was being held, concerning Apartheid.
It was just before dawn.
The rows of moonlit bodies looked like plaster
tempura dishes in the windows of Chez Japan.
The intimate tempura of sleep hid the sushi of youth
& filled the present with the romance of another time,
but inflated slightly like a Hong Kong import.
A lightly spun idea dew plyed lightly the multi-colored polyester,
leaving a dark trench where the speed of commodification
met the definition of symbolic exchange values,
i.e., the labels were inside out,
overturned by nocturnism.
The technical designer stretched in the last ditch of his youth
& rose to embrace the bagels wafting from the bistros.

On the street that morning at about 8:20 A.M.
an ancient man with Pomo D'Oro hair and a sharp
Mephistophelian mustache
was making a telephone call
from a heavily grafittoed booth that had
miraculously preserved a clean southern pane.
He was calling somewhere very far because his lips
formed a small sorrowful noose
like an egg smashed in at the top by a child during
some ancient Easter, soon to be tossed, child and egg,
into the chute of history whence little returns.
I recognized him: it was the lover
of the last Queen of Romania,
a famous playboy of another era.
When I looked, the ancient lover's face cracked:
I saw apologies sucked out of various moonlights
in countries no longer on the map
& he appeared to say, or rather his face did:
"I didn't sleep with her. Very sorry."
But the pomade in his hair said otherwise.

I opened the door of the café
for the belle holding five iced coffees,

who said: "You read my mind."
"It was writ large," I spoke,
"but I'd like to read your body better."
My speech went unnoticed,
having never truly left my throat until this very moment,
but the ancient playboy behind the wall of graffiti,
put his hand over his heart and keeled over,
a vessel of Eros sunk by a phone.
I was the first on the scene
& was reluctant to use the very phone that he . . .
but I did
& paramedics entered the scene in spattered angel suits.
Unbeknownst to anyone I gave him the lover's salute,
silently before the medics came.

In our mutual country several thousand miles to the East
the mad dictator Ceausescu, a triple-chinned gargoyle,
whose place in Hell is being kept by toothless political
prisoners fanning the flames with tracts
(he had once succeeded the man who'd overthrown
the queen the dead man loved)
was ordering the demolition of the ancient capital
to make room for statues of himself.
A 16th-century church gave way to a badly executed bronze head.

I notice that the etiquette of gazing in America's cities
has to do with loss of concentration due to zoning.
The absence or the presence of cafés
is proportioned in direct ratio to gazing eyes.
What looks oblique is really lost
opportunities in real estate.
Other places employ other gazes, terrain-modulated to take in
adventure.
Even the old are only myopically casual:
they too are working for love.
I am tortured by certain looks
I get in dreams from people in my past
who, not content to die and tear a hole in me,
continue staring from beyond.

I find a nervous tropical translation
of those looks in humid cities like New Orleans
or Rio de Janeiro.
In these the dark is moist.
The buildings I would build from the crossings of gazes
by the dead with the living
stand in my mind, blue lines in a blueprint on the immense
glasstop table of a Texas developer.
I would replace the dictator's statues with those.
Besides standing, sheltering, and allowing one to be observed
while seemingly unaware, by one or many,
or to be invisible if one wished,
these buildings would change every hour,
a mix of Persian gardens, Paris cafés, kasbah tents,
Marseille alleys, movable streets, floating flowerbeds,
swaying awnings, and dark dives where to wallow
in the sadness of running out of things to buy.
The passive-poetic of night-day reversal
will enhance the mode of sexy difficulty.
I hope to instill in the construct a feeling
of phones ringing in the steam, and clothes falling
around an ontologically attractive metaphysical node set into the
structure at all levels to make it possible to turn anywhere
one feels the benevolent divine urge of the subject.
What is a subject?
Something that can hold, I expect, for many pages, hours, miles.
Why are your moods so *long?*, someone asked me once.
At the time I barely knew the joys
of the heavenly fifth wind,
where you stand straining the membrane
on the back of all things
against the current of time.
But now when I go into the unknown
I like to travel a few miles.
Everywhere is a new city, everything must be seen at once.
There are, of course, *moments,* peaks where
one story is soldered to the next,
narrative ditches where flattened against the seams
the old demons crouch waiting for sentiment to let them out.

After I left the scene of the death of the lover from the old world,
I took the Greyhound bus to Baton Rouge.
A cowboy was telling a girl about his dog Skipper,
how many times she ran away before she made it,
& about the time he was a welder on board a ship
& a dog kept him prisoner all night one night in Panama,
with a black man who told him about another dog
who jumped after someone who went down in a pond somewhere
in a southern region of the United States known as Dogtown, AL,
& she remembers the day her daddy shot her dog
for biting the village doc whose own dog then took a ear off
Chunky, her own mutt—and the bus didn't rock to a stop,
it growled into the nine dog night
describing a circle that took the welder, me, the bus,
the years, the blueprints of desire, all surrounded
by a thick circle of dogs.
Don't forget, the former ship welder said,
about the girl killed last night in the morning's newspaper
by a mad dog, "prob'ly a nigger or a kike or sumpthin."
"It don't take much for a kid to disappear,"
says the tattooed girl,
a real history of American bad girlhood on her,
blue arrows through red hearts of link chain.
America's wretched riders are arranged by subject matter.
"Dog." "Tattoo." "TV Guide."
There are no foreign students holding Ameripasses.
The front half of the Dawg packs Bibles and guns.
The back half is escapees from institutions,
free-lance murderers, sexual desperadoes,
swamp flowers of genetic damage.
"I left a Bible in a motel in Hollywood,
and now they are making a movie from the parts I underlined,"
my benchmate tells me.
I study the tattoos in front of me.
The pictographs testify to the narrative urge.

Later that month in the avant-garde capital of San Francisco
another movie is being shown.
It is black and white.

Many frames tremble. A girl in one of them opens
a chill window, letting in the fog.
In many frames thereafter she opens the window.
There are also upside down parts in a park.
The girl's knee decked in a deco sock.
A door frame.
The filmmaker explains that he has a birth defect
& that this film essay on love
is proof of a dyslexia from which fountainlike
a plethora of bad decisions have dogged him all his life
until they issued upon the weary frames.
Having committed also lifetimes of them before this life
he sees the sign of healing upon himself in the movement
of the handheld camera, helping him to switch
polarities, so that he might become
that glory of late research, a Left Hander, A South Paw.
To this end, and to hasten its coming,
he does everything with his left,
leaving trails of calligraphed paper
in a childish left hand behind him
in cafés and cinémathèques.

I have a mild dyslexia as well.
An inability to distinguish left from right.
I call it organic anarchism.
It saves time.
But the filmmaker always going left
needs constant readjustment, as he can feel megadoses of vitamins
traveling him like beatniks through the world's *inclinations*
which must be *corrected* by utopia or eternal life,
whichever comes first.
His body is defective, he believes, in places
where it is unfocused on by moral chemistry,
just as reality's defective where the shaky lens is shut.
We, organic anarchists, *au contraire,*
see reality's defects precisely in those places
where art's been stepping in and making scenes.
My hometowns, all of them, are sadly now
overrun by artists who are the churchkeys letting

the tourists out of the sardine cans of the middle class.
Reality's birth defects are magnified by art
until tourists with opera glasses stand
in the pretend infant urine of false representation
looking out into the fake past,
rendered useful to the connoisseur, alas, but lost
to all native sense until retired into a single postcard.
My own childhood town, transformed by reference,
gathers its platonic blueprints into a ball
& rolls into view, there to become a drop containing
a time of pristine transport,
while being, as far as I can tell,
a postcard in the hand of the baffled
tourist who pays dearly for his holograms.
The fake town is redesigned to show even the wear of adoration,
even the places where memory works it over,
tear grooves, canals polished by tongues,
long unsplintered beds dug by stretched index fingers
into the angels pointing at the ceiling of Teutsch Cathedral,
a veritable army of stretched hands and arms.
It would be good
if the shoddy translation job in inferior materials
could stand in contrast to the shining drop in my sometime head.
It's unbelievable how shabby the real Rome is!
Like kept prisoner by a dog on board the working history of the
world.
Poetry plys the rift like a birddog in a mannerist painting.
"Is Mr. Wisdom here?"
"No but mebbe I can find Mr. Stupid for you."
"I am very very sorry to have disturbed you."
"You didn't disturb me. You fucked with my mental *balance!*"

The appropriateness of the locus
of the crime, i.e. "the breaking of the shoe."

Seeing the back of a beautiful girl walking,
I can feel her with my whole body. Amazing.
I must prevent her from turning. It becomes my job.
Maybe she's not a girl at all, but a mailbox, or a newsstand.

Walking behind her down Telegraph Avenue, this lovely Sunday
morn,
I wonder if sex is the opposite of schizo-
phrenia.
Finding myself philosophizing behind her
easy-swinging lovely back, I think to overcome her
and to ask, "Is sex the opposite of schizo-
phrenia?"—
when she turns around,
& smiles at me directly slicing me in half:
"How are you this gorgeous day?"
"Yourself?" I say astonished and inaudible,
meaning her Self as different from her back
which I somehow feel "I know," that it is "mine."
"Oh fine," she says, meaning her back too.
She touches the red frame of my glasses:
"It feels good," she says,
"To take a break from the Eros seminar."

Electromagnetic field reader & manipulator
just inside the gates of my head, shakes his head.
Ah yes the fields exist and they are knowable.
There is nothing bigger than them: not even Time.
But there's a rub: Timing.
I'm on my way to the airport and she's one day late.
The timing of knowledge is the crux.
But in her crux time is made right.
The crux is always present to the crucial.
Mistimed knowledge lines the pits
the true originals lie in becoming drops.
But there was never a time when things could have been different.
They are always different.
Does uselessness invalidate seeing?
Should schizos be protected like brujos or restored like vases?
In the sexualized field, analysis (chemistry) encounters action (faith)
for purposes of reassessing the description.
The tearing of the veils,
the breaking of the crust,
are immediately followed by the blinding

revelation of organic
complexity underneath.
To make another whole it is necessary to remake all the parts.
Which are themselves wholes formed of further particulars.
There is no self-generated
return to the surface
because there is no "self."
The fragmented cluster of particulars
in a state of rapid disintegration
whirls by in search of a matching cluster
& is further pulled apart.
Violence from the outside has certain advantages
if the object to be put
back together
serves some function in that state.
Should I now fall apart
I am doubtful if enough
usefulness could be found in me——
barring discovery of the drops—
to justify
bringing me back to one unit.
Better to mark each part with the word Taboo.
But if you're sexy enough they'll name a perfume after you.

At the truck stop where America's last free storks nest,
a killer leaves a Popeye's chicken box.
Inside it is the hand of formerly his best friend.
The former welder on the bus retches and smokes dust.
The ship's cook once made nail clipping soup.
For one hundred bucks Greyhound is good forever.
"We haven't been off the bus for eight years,
except to buy Popeye's." Sunsets, sunrises,
nausea-lined faces form solidly into a coffin bashing
rudderless against the TV.
We on the other side let's wave at the lumpenproletariat.
Sooner will sulfates cyanide silicon selenium salt
go through the eye than minor psychos into America.
Who remembers Juan Corona?
Gacey?

Whitman of Texas?
Ng and the Chowchilla boys?
Where is the handsome Black Doodler
with his sketches of soon-to-die lovers?
The Zodiac Killer who scratched his stars on corpses?
Charles Manson of the Beatle-mysteriumed Bacchae?
Miller of Atlanta, bridges, strangled children, night?
Where are the newspapers of yore?
The ship of gore?
Scuzz, scum, flotsam, dusted, juiced, sick,
the Dark goes Greyhound and Big Red, and hitches
toward the TV glass.
Wave harder now.
There used to be a way through the glass,
some of the old timers remember.
You could hitch a ride through literachoor.
Why, there was Kerouac.
You could go through him right up to America
& it was like you'd always been there.
Well, half in and half outta da glass at least.
There useta be a mesh of coincidence right about here,
& conjecture, riding the narrative folds to some under-
standing of eros in liberty, and then it was a short hike
home.
I'm looking, but for what?
It's been mended.
There is a preacher in the hole collecting a junk army:

Halleluja brothers & Hosanna!
It was a dark hour when they put him in the grave.
It was Friday!
But Sunday is here!
They don't celebrate Easter in Poland today like we do
They have the jackboot on their neck!
It's Friday in Poland!
But Sunday is coming!
The Soviets are strafing villages in Afghanistan
Killing women & children
It's Friday in Afghanistan!
But Sunday is coming!

And Napoleon was broken at Waterloo
Where he kept hitting and hitting
But Wellington's line wouldn't break!
Two thousand years ago Satan threw everything he had at Jesus
But the rock didn't break!
And today godless Communism throws everything against
the rock of faith & the rock doesn't break!
And the media knows not an iota of the Gospels!
One day is coming when you'll turn on your TV & only the voice
of the Gospels be coming through!
It's Friday in the world
But Sunday is Coming!

The drama of Eros and Self goes on in the pews
where the cross-eyed folk wink at each other.

Back in Berkeley, California, I am given a starring role
In the Opera Bouffe of Exile!
A million forgotten ideas fight for my ear.
I sing the part of the Ear.
My fellow wanderers want my ear.
No, no, I say, what you want is America's Eye!
But they are all stubborn like my mother.
"Since she became a cyclop, we had no rest, your mother
and I . . ."
There are ministers without portfolios singeing their barbered
whiskers on a violence without victims . . .
Academics without chairs, desks, carcels, universities . . .
Monarchists without a king tripping on the red carpet of the
hotel lobby with vials of blood in their palsied pockets
from which they furtively sip as their wrinkles briefly
disappear . . .
Fascists without leaders, fuehrerless fanatics . . .
Nudists dressed in the armor of discarded truths . . .
Icon painters falling to their knees with heavy wooden crosses
about their meaty necks . . .
The very lover of Queen Marie who has reappeared with his
plasterboard
hair wandering all over the map of our vanished country,
carving new valleys of Vitalis broadcasting yellowed

instructions and codes carrying from phone booth to phone
booth that sickle-thin fin-de-siècle smile
that says always, forever, I didn't really, besides
it wasn't any good, it was a literary idea, she was
a writer you know . . .
but no book will ever be about us?
I see ideologues of splinters of splinters
arranged in tiers, a political cake of parties
on frayed tablecloths in unrestored European hotels
waiting for the beringed fingers of a native autocracy
to plunge through the icing for a taste of their hearts.
Arranged arachnid-style around the chandeliers
are painters of icons "in the traditional manner"
waiting for a signal to descend upon the cake flames
which are tall Orthodox silver crosses
shaking aromatic powder or the dust of the IXth Arondissement.
They have traveled long distances to praise God,
& have some cake, have some cake.
God is everywhere an occasion for a gâteau-da-fé.
But perhaps they all wait for muscle, not for religion.
For young punks to back up the bitter yeast of their spectacular
escapes from everywhere into the story
no one wants to hear, alas. Like tremulous
and not-so-young mademoiselles from another century,
refined beyond present-day understanding,
they speak 25 languages & not one of them the vulgate.
The hotel's tarnished gilded salon trembles during the verse-
recitation
of the boring epic,
wishing it was listening to Charles Baudelaire instead.
Everything desuete & lost is in the dusty escritoires,
shorted violetas, misclustered chandeliers.
I meet a young woman here. In the shade of her violent eye make-up
are her recent memories when with 13 of her friends
she lay in front of the President's limousine,
her hi-heeled shoes pointing an ultimatum at the spiky
tyrant in his Brooks Brothers blazer & Calvin Klein jeans,
as her high-placed family trembled awaiting the phonecall
from the secret police.

In my day a certain gentleness still attached to the electrodes,
a multithreaded rag of innuendos especially licensed
by one's lycée to pass themselves off as metaphors.
Brutality hadn't quite become art for art's sake.
I meet a great critic.
After 5 years in prison,
he is only interested in California boys.
They say, he tells me, that this is the capital
of perverted sex! I am a FEROCIOUS pervert!
They have diseases here,
an alarmed dissident folklorist tells him.
They might catch something from *me*, shouts the critic,
& the pathos of lost diseases shines briefly
in cot B of his former cell,
political, historical, intellectual diseases that flare
in his joints and at the seams of the world's wounds giving
the critic's eyes a certain flaming luster.
What is a virus to those?
Places where folk die of philosophy
don't share geography with places where people die of diseases.
They share no air, no words, no maps.
Three to a room, they're kept
waiting for people to enter & tear
apart in interesting patterns.
I am conversing with the chief exspook from America's
Secret Radio Police who is about to break the news
to me that I make a lousy Ear
when the lobby fills suddenly with humans in wheelchairs,
torsos on skateboards,
arms in slings,
steel hooks,
bandanas over deep body holes.
The chief says, "Here is the next convention,
they booked them one day early, there will be a mess."
Exile has its internal tourist attractions and a timetable out of wack.
Mistimed etc. lines the pits etc.
I watch my countrymen carrying an unfair argument with the ghosts
trapped in their memory drops, and I wish
I could rain on them to take them home.

The old country and their youth are intact in the blue atmosphere
around each and every one of them,
& they are ready to die for it.
Some would do double duty and also die for art.
I stand astonished at the certainty of what art.
A bouquet of little indulgences waits crammed in the jewel box
of my memory to be pried ajar by my fellow exiles.
I enter the escritoire of meta-finances, filled to the transoms
with hotel bills and laundry tickets,
& looks at the many cities below
unchanged in the geography of desire:
Vienna, Buenos Aires, Tangiers, Paris, London, New York, and
Caracas.
They are my mantilla's arousal, my calling card,
this premier assent of cities of exile into the heart
of my explicative genius at its flood-season height.
A drop would suffice to render understanding unto all
but the operation is not visual, not designed for a flat Eros,
though it is a little shabby
like Spain maybe before the Conquest.
What can't be had is worth equipping an armada for.
What is invisible always has a door.
A solid brass door encrusted hopefully with the eyes of romance.
It's Berkeley, Brazil, Lima, Bangkok, or France.
The esprit of despair takes poets by the throat to produce
not a Classical Age but a holding pattern, a sterling fork
to tune the streets for better holding forth.
I am breathing through one hundred straws,
each one designed to suck in another *paysage*
& I am bleeding through eight hundred little wounds
each one mined by an expatriate's *vernissage*
which is why when they hold me a certain angle like an ear,
in the sun, I am a copper sieve sifting red flour on
piles of little uncirculated shiny coins labeled *Mnemogasoline Drops*.
Royalties on the books that result thereof are paid by the wind,
alone among the elements to read.
The whirring of iridescent scholarly beetles bores the light.
I did set out to be an icon, it's true.
The people in my village wished fervently for it,

even though I was born in a rather large city,
& always had the lowest opinion of hicks—even when,
I shamefully confess, the Lord lowered his rifle on the peasants
& had them made first into dust, then into symbols.
I became a sort of icon I called The Sword and The Mascara.
There are no watchers, of course, and this is good.
It would be fine if there were watchers who knew that the watched
were hiding something even if it was only their artificiality
which made them act that way.
Which way is that?

The victims of art are now simply called citizens.
They display their victimization
like a passport to civilization.
Their formal bodies are art. I mean, mine is.
We stand between the books and cannot be told apart.
If we are picked up we open everywhere and can be read quickly.
We stand in galleries mournfully unable to look as modern as that.
We walk out of the pages of books and back on the streets
lined with epochal reminder craft just like the entries we mean
to stay in when our bodies go.
We are enticing but there aren't any observers.
Who can stand outside to say Ah?

The problem with autobiography
is that you find yourself in places already written up.
The world takes on an insufferable literary air.
Everybody's in it & they are always home.
There is a volume of déjà vu.
Even if you have changed things ever so slightly.
The déjà vu is distorted ever so literally,
reality takes on that defective air,
a defect of translation passing for a defect of birth.
The shadows of the defective turn on their hinges,
tarnished by reference to adoration & translation.
Say what? Say what? Repetition is not exact?
Hence realism's impossible?
Even by the barbed wire of native innocence?
The world believes in sex, the absurd, and gymnastics,

& I *could* to keep it at that,
but even with my back to the beautiful girl I can still
plot her abduction from fertile mythos
in inexact replication of every situation.
"Beautiful back, beautiful, sinuous, grace-driven back,
with only primitive political ideas,
a great curved organ for paradox, called 'spine,'
I'm going to caress you with my breath, in time with your fifth
unliterary sense, with my rainbow brush!"
I would not mind being leaned against your back and shot!
Viva to All That!
Believe me, I would. The fields are real, they are knowable, they
exist, there is nothing bigger than them,
not even our two human bosses: Mister Time & Comrade Timing.
It is not as a poet I speak but as a pedestrian & a boy.
People, love your waitresses and your bus drivers,
& the veins that run from the back of the bus
where the crazies retch,
to the front where the depressed
think everything is their fault,
& the paranoiacs
that nothing is.
Oh, sad is their song!

SAVING THE BOAT PEOPLE

JOE DAVID BELLAMY

Leslie's Journal—Nov. 23rd—Arrival
The Lieus, a Cambodian family, emerged from the Air North commuter, slowly, timidly, all wearing the same Army surplus T-shirts and enormous yellow numbered badges on their shoulders and backs. They must have been sorted out and numbered like cattle in the refugee camps. Now they looked like figures from some absurd game of human bingo, which, in a sense, they were, numbered not for the slaughter but for the opportunity to begin new lives; and, pathetically, the four children were barefoot and the adults, Mr. and Mrs. Lieu and the elderly grandmother, wore only cheap thongs on their feet, though the temperature hovered in the mid-forties.

The small welcoming group—Mr. Kennedy, the Methodist minister, the three other concerned village women, and I, clucking and smiling and making every effort to communicate welcome and brotherhood—quickly engulfed them and ushered the Lieus into the satisfactory heat of the waiting van.

Saang
The metallic craft brought them to the earth again, and through the plastic curtain she glimpsed a barren, desolate landscape more terrifying than any dream and all the color of death. The humans also were the color of death, the most hideous beings she had ever seen, like large pale slugs walking upright, waving their swollen limbs,

94

and baring their teeth strangely, as if upset or in pain. Surrounded by the giant pale-people, who resembled the enemy who had killed them, they were miserably frightened; and the landscape also was a horrible disappointment. The white air hurt their skins it was so white. How such creatures could feed their bodies from the dry, hard land was a mystery to her. They seemed peaceful, but whenever they approached them, they showed their teeth like sick dogs and spoke an ugly language at them and one to another. "If the great fat male seizes my arm," she told herself, "I must not cry out." The baby began to wail uncontrollably as soon as he set eyes on the crowd of deathly faces hovering above him.

Leslie
She does her stretching on the porch, laying her heel on the snow-scalloped railing and reaching for her pointed toe, then the other leg. Then the quads—catching her foot from behind, pushing it up her back. Bouncing on her toes, leaving a filigree of Nike tread-marks pressed into the powdery floorboards like the fossilized track of some as-yet-undiscovered species.

Out into the quiet snowy street, taking short quick easy steps, as unobtrusive as a fox, just any middle-aged woman out jogging, correctly dressed, easily identifiable as—a jogger. Nothing desperate, sexual, or escapist about this, not at all. What could be a more socially sanctioned activity—twenty million people out here on the roads and walkways of the nation running off the pounds, thinning out the blood; and she is a part of it, the great running craze. A still living representative of all those people from previous generations who used to carry the load of heavy physical labor in the culture, all the really good fieldhands and cartwrights and farmers and lumberjacks, the ones who were in some way sustained by the daily sweat and toil and fatigue of it and had passed on their genes to her—they were causing it, their instincts, their inheritance, their needs, finding expression through her body.

Beyond the rows of houses, she cuts down the familiar rutted country road, blue with snow and etched with the narrow runnels of cross-country ski-blades. In the fall, this trail was thick with ragweed and goldenrod and Queen Anne's lace, the air spicy with the scents of pollen and newmown hay. Now it is overlaid with white, the brownish stalks poking out above the crust, the only visible remnants of the dense vegetable spawning; and the air pinches the nostrils and nearly takes her breath away.

Her accident was . . . two years ago this fall, and she would never be the same. Tears spread back across her temples like the feathers on a bird's wing. No snow then—cars splashing trails of mist, slick asphalt, bubbles of drops clinging to the thick roadside grass like a coating of jewels, the rusty pickup perpetually zooming down upon her like an avenging beast, the two unknown distorted faces gaping in the windshield. They had actually driven off the road to hit her. It had happened so suddenly she couldn't remember or hadn't seen what their faces might have revealed of their motives—contempt for joggers, hatred of women, random homicidal idiocy, drunken frenzy, or merely a slip of the wheel—she guessed she would never know, though she could never stop thinking about it. No motive—no motive at all—seemed plausible to her.

The blow spun her against the cab, where she struck the crown of her head, and then flipped her into the mushy loam of a cornfield, where, when she awoke, she was staring up from the base of several gigantic stalks and the tassles overhead seemed to race across the sky like the traffic above an airport. Her rescuers carried her for miles, it seemed, up a cliff of pastureland toward the glowing lights of a dairy barn. She could neither walk nor speak and, by then, the pickup was long gone. She thinks she remembers all of this exactly, but it may have been a dream—she lay in critical condition in a coma for four weeks and three operations, including brain surgery. She was to become a statistic, an official victim, and the subject of a stern editorial in the local paper about the need for additional caution among both joggers and motorists if such tragic accidents were not to become commonplace. She recovered, more or less, but the process was slow and painful, and the accident left her with a minor speech defect, not an easy thing to accept for someone with her previous verbal skills and energies. It is this incident, and its aftermath, her husband Jerry says, that give Leslie such a "unique capacity to empathize with suffering humanity, with victims of every sort."

Another mile or so and she will have exhaled as much of Jerry's Benson & Hedges pollution as she is likely to get rid of in one day's struggling, the superficial layers only, and already she is imagining with powerful vividness the desperate little alveoli in her lung tissue, each like a small choking mouth gasping for air and slowly, inexorably, filling up with a pool of tar like a dark tear.

Saang

The larger woman has eaten the food of many people; yet, she seems not to be troubled by this. Her arms are as thick as four arms, perhaps five arms. And there are others like her, many others. Even the thin people, like Less-lee, are so robust, so well-fleshed. Where would they find the harvests, the abundance for such heavy eating in this barren land? Where do they find the food to fatten even their dogs? Each family in the village keeps a fattened dog as if to boast of their excesses. My very dog is fatter than your very dog. What can this mean?

Yesterday, we were taken to a building called the Supper-Market, where they had piled food to the ceilings in every row. So many little colored boxes, and bright lights shining from every corner of the room. Huge tables covered with slabs of red meat many layers together, enough to feed us all for months! As quickly as the people remove the goods from the shelf or table, men in white gowns rush forward from behind the butcher-door to replenish those very items. At first I thought they must have a very huge warehouse in back of the butcher-door, but if so, it is nowhere visible from the exterior. I often worry about what may be behind the butcher-door at the Supper-Market.

We have brought home so many sacks of food, it required two of the wire carts to transport them to the Ford. We have taken perhaps too much for our share and the people might realize now that we eat too much and send us back to the Thai camps. I cannot comprehend why they would want to give us so much food at once right at the beginning before they have seen us work. I sometimes have a very deep fear that they are fattening us all up for some purpose I do not wish to think of.

Leslie

In the early stages of her negotiations with the church, Leslie received an anonymous phone call during which she was told that if she insisted on pursuing her idea about bringing refugees to the village, one day she might come home and find a pile of charred rubble where her house used to be.

"First it was the Blacks in this country, wanting a free ride, now the Cubans and Mexicans and Chinks. Every refugee you bring in, it takes a job away from a legalized citizen. Don't you do-gooders understand that?" He hung up before she had a chance to reply—just some miserable and ignorant hungover man who wanted to express an opinion. She wasn't ready to take his threat seriously, but it did make her more sensitive about public opinion and her obligation to persuade people of the rightness of what she was doing. One day in the grocery store she overheard someone in the next aisle saying, "Why can't we just send the money to the refugees and let them stay in their own country? For God's sake, why do we have to bring them over here? This is too far north for them. They'll never fit in here." Leslie hurried around the row of shelving and confronted the two women: "Look," she said, "they've la-la-lost their country. Th-th-th-there's no place but here for them to go." On her way home, she passed a pickup with a gun rack across the back window and a bumper sticker that read: "Hungry—eat your foreign car." It was a bad day.

She knows the unspeakable, the unarguable, the crushing fact is—Jerry no longer finds her sexually attractive since the accident. He no longer sleeps with her. Lately, he has begun discussing the social and philosophical merits of open marriage. The sense of alienation is almost palpable and getting worse, and she doesn't know why this has happened. She is the same person, isn't she? He seems upset by her running, by her refugee project, by everything that gives meaning to her life. He disguises his contempt for her under a cloud of solicitous concern. "Hadn't you better just take it easy for a while longer?" "Let someone else save the boat people. Why does it have to be us? We have our own problems." Or, after two cocktails, "If you hadn't gone to that silly liberal school, maybe you wouldn't have turned into such an insufferable bleeding heart."

In fact, he is such a prude, he is undoubtedly embarrassed by her running and, also, by the public exposure of her rescue project. He doesn't like the idea of *his* wife appearing all around town in nothing but her sheer nylon running briefs or her wet-look Gortex and sweatband like a savage, ecstatically pumping endorphins. Or maybe he doesn't want her to reveal her sweating thighs or cheeks, in case his golf or drinking buddies might be watering their lawns or shoveling their driveways at a particular hour. But, surely, if he knows *anything* about her, if he has learned one single truth about her character after fifteen years of marriage, he should know that she *must* continue to run, after what has happened to her, she *must* do it, and she must carry her rescue project through to completion. It is not merely the result of "misdirected maternal instinct," as he has claimed, that she feels compelled to contribute to the relief effort. How absurd! The greatest amateur psychologist of our time always has a conveniently pathological explanation these days for all her motives and hopes.

Leslie's Journal, Dec. 1st
Impressions during first few days: The house seemed to please the Lieus, though they are obviously still confused and distracted from their long ordeal. The small, white clapboard house is on a quiet street, Elm Street in the village, and the rental is being supported by donations from the community and the churches, though the churches have been somewhat less helpful than I might have imagined. We have enough to keep the house for only four months—a fact I am keeping to myself—and I am counting heavily on the further generosity of concerned members of the area and the appeal of the Lieus' presence itself to generate other contributions to their overall support. In an emergency, the small side-porch might be rented out as a separate apartment to help defray expenses, though at present it seems best not to complicate the Lieus' adjustment by inviting strangers to live so nearby. These people deserve privacy and quiet and space after the anguish they have endured. Eventually, we must find work for Mr. Lieu. We must find other, better ways to stimulate people's altruistic impulses. This is our personal contribution to the betterment of humanity, an individual, manageable portion of the world's affliction. We must see that these helpless, frightened little people can survive and prosper.

Further impressions: Though the language barrier is such a problem for all of us, we are slowly growing to understand the Lieus. When we returned from the grocery today, for instance, I was especially touched by Mr. Lieu's behavior. The man refused to eat until after all the children had been fed. (I wonder how often he has gone hungry?) We, of course, tried to convince him that there was enough food for everyone. But then we began to see that it was a matter of principle with him. Eventually, he did eat a small portion of Minute Rice.

Later, I was equally surprised by little Koki. When Judy Wheeler and I began to comb the little girl's hair, the hair kept coming out in alarming tufts in the comb. Finally we smoothed it out and clipped it with a small barrette and held Koki up to show her how she looked in the bathroom mirror. I've never seen such a look of astonishment on anyone's face. It was almost as if she had never seen herself in a mirror before that moment. At other times, she has a deep, pensive look, a look too old, too experienced, for her small face. I suppose the most horrible sight that most of the local children have ever seen is, say, a nightcrawler squashed on the sidewalk or something unreal from a horror film. But these Cambodians, those little dark eyes, oh, my!—what *they* have seen I hate to *think* what they have seen.

Leslie

During her run, Leslie determines to try to improve things with Jerry. She will go by the office, she decides, and make a point of asking what he would like for dinner. She will be wifely and caring and see how he responds. Around five, she jogs to campus and into his building at the top of the quad. The halls are deserted at this hour. The students have wandered off to the dining halls, and the professors have all gone home, except for *her* husband. The fact that he is still here strikes her as additional evidence of his alienation from her rather than as proof of any special resolution on his part or dedication to his work. He doesn't *want* to come home. He would rather be here in this empty building, smoking and grading composition themes or taking a leisurely gander at the *New York Times*, as if the *New York Times* could tell him anything essential about his life or about their lives together. A wave of self-pity bends her mouth as she moves lightly up the steps to the second floor, trying to nurture a sense of buoyancy she does not really feel.

The door to his office is slightly open, and she sees immediately that he is, in fact, not alone. Someone wearing a shapely pair of ankle-strap pumps is sitting across from him, swinging her foot ever so slightly below her crossed legs. Leslie stops abruptly, out of sight, focusing on the arrogance and presumed familiarity of the gesture, puzzled at first, then alarmed that she might be seen, either by Jerry and the girl in the office with him, or by somebody coming unexpectedly down the hall, where she would be seen standing, appearing to eavesdrop. "I'm not taking anything for granted," the girl is saying.

"I'm not either," Jerry says. "I know I *like* having you around, Debbie. If you think I'm going to be turned off by your silly cock-teasing games, you're wrong."

"That wasn't the idea," the girl is saying, "not at all."

Leslie sways quickly back the way she came in and flees softly and quietly down the stairs and out of the building into the chilly anonymous darkness of snowplowed walks, where she pretends to be jogging again with some definite destination in mind, bouncing up and down foolishly like some frisky adolescent, as her pounding heart takes a nose dive. If she runs far enough now, her mind will be a large empty window, a vastness of rolling white like the moonlit fields outside of town at midnight, and she will not have to feel or think anything about what she has just seen and heard. She will not have to feel or think anything at all.

Saang
We grew and harvested acres of rice, but the crop was collected by Pol Pot's soldiers and hauled away. The Khmer Rouge told the people in Siem Reap they were sending the rice to Battambang. But in Battambang they collected the rice and told the people there they were sending it to Siem Reap. We never knew why all the rice had disappeared. Some days we had to divide one cup of rice fragments among a hundred people. We ate grass and roots and mice and insects. We saw which flowers the horses ate—and we ate flowers. We were desperate for food. We ate like animals. Some turned into animals. I know mothers who ate their dead babies. Almost everyone ate human flesh.

There was a madman in the village who always had a secret supply of meat. My mother used to trade tobacco and gold with him for a few pieces of fat to add to our soup. One day Pol Pot's soldiers broke into this man's house. There were more than sixty human corpses inside—some partially carved up and still bloody and covered with flies—and piles of bones stacked about the rooms and an enormous wealth of gold and trade goods. While the children of our village looked on, the Khmer Rouge beat the man to death until his skull was a pulp on the floor. Then they looted the dwelling and burned every trace of it with flame-throwing rifles.

If we had not escaped this madness, we would surely have perished or gone insane. In the darkness of night in the United States, I often remember the small boat that transported us across the Mekong to Nong Khai—its very drift and creak. We had walked for five days and nights. We feared the fisherman would awake and discover us as we pushed his boat into the dark waters. My sister, Vathana, had been shot to death in such a place, her body poured out on the bank of the river, where the family later came to cremate her, chanting somber prayers and weeping. Therefore, Vathana was much in my mind as we floated across the Mekong that night. The body of my small brother Koy, who also tried to leave with Vathana, has never yet been found. I imagined that the face of young Koy was there too beside Vathana's under the current. Other dead bodies were already swimming there and brushed against our low bow, soft and horrible as squid, or perhaps some were only branches or debris in the black waters, though they seemed to be begging to crawl in with us. When the baby began to cry, I stuffed his mouth full of rags to muffle the sound. I hardly recall the landing or how we later came to the camp, only the groaning of the boards of that small, clumsy boat, the mist, and the frightening quiet and the stillness of the souls upon the water.

Later, I learned that—as punishment for our escape—my relatives were killed by the Khmer Rouge, more than forty people—my father and mother, all my remaining sisters and brothers, uncles and cousins. All were murdered or starved to death. I and my children are the only members of my family left in the world.

In the morning light, we left the boat in the tall grass, collected our few belongings, and walked off down the long road. We had eaten nothing in the three days, and could barely walk, and were without rice, fish, silk or gold for trade. As we came near to the Thai camp, we heard shouts in the distance and, slowly ahead, as in a mirage, hordes of men, dressed all in blue jeans and blue-jean jackets and wearing cowboy hats, were yelling excitedly and holding up chickens for sale by their scaly feet and plastic blow-dryers and French perfume bottles and boxes of Thai cigarettes at $20 each pack.

Leslie

Leslie is running quickly along the village streets on this cold, clear night after nine, a slender figure in a dark blue running suit with silver reflective stripes. The points of the heels of her running shoes are also reflective, so that whenever a vehicle approaches within a certain distance of her, its headlights arc back from her moving body and the driver sees a luminescent figure advancing or fading away, its limbs glowing or sparkling eerily, like some heavenly or extraterrestrial visitation.

Leslie's Journal
The children have been sick for several days now, especially little Koki, and I have spent the last two nights looking after them, sleeping on the side-porch and getting up in the wee hours to sponge their foreheads, take temperatures, spoon out medicine, and comfort them. The symptoms are cramps, abdominal upsets, fevers, and sweats. Saang has these same symptoms too, sometimes even more severe, in fact; but, according to Dr. Goldberg, it is nothing but an array of intestinal parasites they most likely picked up in the Thai camps, where the sanitary conditions are so notoriously poor.

Unfortunately, their condition did cause a problem at school. Some of the local children started making fun of Koki and the others when they would double up in agony and run for the restroom. Young children can sometimes be brutally cruel. Several of the teachers were concerned that whatever the Lieu children have might be contagious. Hepatitis and typhoid fever have been mentioned in rumors and have led to a certain amount of pointless hysteria.

Update: Saang and the children have responded well to treatment and are feeling much better now. This will be my last night on the side-porch, and I am almost sorry to leave. Why is it that helping these people seems so important and so gratifying to me? Taking the medicine in to Saang last night, as she rose up out of the covers and waited for me to pour the syrup into the spoon, I noticed for the first time really how exceptional her face is, how truly beautiful she might be when her health returns. It is a benign, exotic beauty, like that of some forlorn and forgotten, almond-eyed Asian princess, and almost frightening when one considers how far she has come to this place and under what circumstances and, by contrast, how alien and ugly we must seem to her. What can she possibly think of us?

Leslie's Journal (cont.)
We have been fortunate to secure work for Mr. Lieu—Kyheng—as a dishwasher at the Evergreen Inn. The salary is not much, but it should certainly help; and, more importantly, it should help give

the Lieus a greater sense of self-sufficiency and involvement in the life of the community. Also, it will inevitably cause the people of the town to appreciate the sort of industrious, deserving family they have brought into their midst. The Lieus want to make their own way. They have a resilience and determination that is remarkable to behold. I'm sure they will be an asset to the town, and their story might make it easier to resettle other refugees in locations such as ours.

Language is the hardest ongoing problem. Judy Wheeler tutors Mr. Lieu three times a week, but his progress has not been as swift as that of Saang and the children. He is by temperament a very shy, private man. Because of that fact and the nature of his work, he will have little opportunity to practice what he has learned. If he is ever going to find better work, however, which I am sure he is capable of eventually, he will need to know more English.

Leslie

Leslie often spends evenings with the Lieu family. Kyheng, who has spent the day washing dishes at the Evergreen Inn, is now finishing up the dinner dishes. He reminds her of a porpoise—his hands splashing in the water and the dark gleam of his hair. At the same time, the stiff formality of his face and neck is very unlike a porpoise. Once, when she was trying to explain a joke to him, he suddenly understood—either what she was saying or the essence of it—and his face was transformed by crow's-feet into a look of boyish hilarity.

Someone from the Church has donated a small black-and-white television set for the Lieus, saying, "This will help them learn the language and give them quicker insights into American culture." Leslie is not so sure these are insights they wouldn't be better off without, but she has delivered the set and helped show them how to turn it on and adjust it. The Lieus seem quite amazed and grateful. Apparently, they had never seen a TV set up close before.

Leslie sits quietly in the darkened living room admiring the little family as they watch their TV set. She has made this possible. They are such innocent, deserving people, and such a close-knit family. Saang and Kyheng are particularly close. Occasionally Leslie has seen the two of them in town, on the street together, has seen the way they have of sharing a look without uttering a word. But, after all, they are strangers in a strange land and have no other face, no other responsible person (except her) to turn to and share a feeling. She can sometimes feel the spirit that must be between them. She envies it. She does not envy them their fates—of course not that—but she does envy them for their closeness and selflessness.

When she leaves, they are watching a rerun of *Jaws*. She hopes it will not give them nightmares. They are so hypnotically involved that they hardly notice she is walking out the door.

Saang
The large fish with many teeth tries to eat the people. The picture of the fish was taken while it was swimming in the Atlantic Ocean. The picture was piped into a tower and propelled out into the air over many miles. The picture slides through the clouds alongside the several airplanes until it arrives into the plastic window of our TV network box. All of the people who swam in the Atlantic Ocean were eaten or killed by the huge fish, which is larger than a boat.

Leslie
After two miles, her legs feel ripe with blood, flushed and taut, and her movement as lubricated and smooth as a well-oiled engine. But she is not an engine. She is flesh and blood, warm, palpable, living. A living thing. A living creature, running now along a country road with a primitive sense of freedom as the wind blows against her face. A person, like any other, somewhat better educated and focused than most perhaps, somewhat more determined to impose her will upon the world—the inert, blind, stubborn, pitiful world. But *no more deserving* for the luck of possessing brains and an expensive background—not at all. *More responsible*. A duty to serve the good of the species as a whole. "Be ashamed to die until you have won some victory for humanity." She knows the human significance of these words. She understands them at some organic or cellular level. Her life is posed in a precarious balance, waiting to fulfill this particular mission or calling—to perform some act of charity or devotion large enough to qualify as a victory for humanity.

Saang
The sick woman has a pill in her hand, and after eating it she feels much better. Many very happy people drink Coke, and beer delivered by horses with huge feet. Several men like to shave their

faces with buffalo curd. Then they run back and forth bouncing a ball and shouting at one another.

Leslie

The waitress takes Leslie's order to the kitchen, where Kyheng is visible behind the counter. He does not notice her in the dining room. He seems to be racing someone to see who can finish the dishes first. Occasionally, he growls sideways, or seems to, though no one is there. Then his eyes return to his hands, bloodless in the scalding water. The boss likes him, the waitress tells Leslie, because, besides being a hard worker, he never complains and never flinches or talks back when being yelled at. The waitress does not know of Leslie's connection to Mr. Lieu. She thinks Leslie is just curious. "Sometimes around happy hour, some of the men get after him," the waitress says. "They call him Small Pot. They don't like it that he has a job and some of them don't. But Lou"—Lou, she calls him—"doesn't pay any attention. He just smiles away and keeps on washing dishes. I think he understands a lot more than people give him credit for," the waitress says. "I think it's a wonderful thing that he came to this country to be free like the rest of us."

After she finishes her lunch, Leslie goes to the kitchen to say hello to Kyheng. She is relieved when he gives her a toothy grin and seems honored to see her. She lays her arm in a maternal way around his shoulders and starts to say something fatuous about the dishes when suddenly she finds she is crying heavily into the moist neck of his shirt and he is clutching a dripping cup against her sweater, blinking in surprise, and trying hastily to back away and detach himself.

Saang

I use a tub and washboard from the church people to clean our clothes. The water flows from the spigot already hot, and the suds from the box are thick and full of foam. The strange fragrance from the powerful soap hurts the nostrils. My fingers become red in the scalding soapiness. I rush to hang the clothes on the line before darkness enfolds. My hands grow stiff in the white air, pinning up the wash I can barely see. In the morning, when I go out in the yard to collect these very same clothes, I scream. The shirts and dresses and pants have turned to plastic in the night, or perhaps it is white wood. They are glued to the rope, and when I pull them away, the plastic breaks and falls in small knives across my wrists. I run inside sobbing to tell Kyheng that our clothes have been forever ruined.

When Less-lee knocks, I tell her dreadfully of the mishap of the clothesline. She understands and is never angry. It will be all right, Less-lee says. We must take the clothes to a place called the Laundry-mat, she says, in the wintertime. She goes outside to look, and we put the hard clothes into a basket and into the backseat of her Ford.

The Laundry-mat is a large room with rows of white plastic machines and round windows in the walls, like the ones of the airplane, looking out onto a dark hole, and the burning smell of soap, ticklish in my nose. Together, Less-lee and I unsnap the airport window and fold the clothes into what seems a sideways tub. Less-lee puts coins into it, and suddenly the clothes begin to turn and bounce and the machine makes a rumbling. Less-lee squeezes my shoulder and we stand together a long time and watch the hard clothes jump inside the airport door.

Leslie

The doorbell rings and Jerry goes to answer it. He stands for several minutes jawing with someone in the doorway.

"Who is it?" Leslie says, assuming it is one of his students, maybe the girl from his office.

"Old Professor Henry can't find his cat. Have you seen it?"

"No."

"He thought you might have seen it out on the trails somewhere, jogging along."

"Very funny. No, ba-but tell him I'll keep an eye out for it."

He returns to the door and talks further with Mr. Henry. The old man is a retired English professor who lives across the street. He wears a trench coat and a beret and walks his overweight, beige-haired cat on a string and secretly encourages it to defecate in the yards of neighbors who are not at home. When the cat escapes, he hunts for it with desperate determination; but the cat always comes back eventually.

Later that day, Leslie jogs over to Elm Street to visit the Lieus. Her legs are strong and eager and the short run feels good. The sun is out, bright on the fresh snow, and the yards shine as if encrusted with tiny diamonds. The Lieus are bustling about in their kitchen, looking happier than she has seen them in some time. An odd smell fills the house, and Kyheng smilingly shows her some hideous thing, something not-quite-chickenlike roasting in the oven. "Where did you ge-get it?" Leslie says to Kyheng, uneasily. "Where did the meat ca-ca-come from?" Kyheng looks to Saang for help with an answer.

"He catch," Saang says. "Set trap for small animal." Saang points proudly to a curl of bloody beige hair resting in a newspaper on the countertop. The truth of the matter hits Leslie with a sickening sense of certainty.

"Oh, my God," she says.

"We save money," Saang says.

"Oh, no," Leslie says. "This is a mistake. You must not tra-trap animals in town. Ma-many people have small animals as pets. They will not approve of it, and there are laws against tra-tra-trapping in town. This is something Kyheng must not do e-ever again."

"Not in our country," Saang says.

"But in this country it is so. It is believed very strongly. I will have to explain what has ha-happened to the man who owns this cat. He will be very angry."

Saang addresses Kyheng, explaining about the cat. The expression on his face goes from openness to astonishment to abject regret and guilt. He babbles something incomprehensible to Leslie and rushes to the oven, throws open the door, and pulls out the pan with the cat-carcass, burning his hands and slamming it into the counter. The cat rolls out of the pan just as Kyheng releases the hot metal handles and drops everything with a crash in the middle of the kitchen linoleum and then quickly turns and runs cold water over his hands from the nearby spigot. He stands there, shaking his wet hands like fluttering birds over the sink, afraid to look at anything but the cat-carcass and pan in the middle of the floor. He is the picture of a contrite man, and Leslie can't help feeling sorry for him, though she turns away, suddenly queasy in her stomach. Saang, scolding Kyheng loudly in her native language, begins to pick up the mess, carefully using a folded dishrag as she bends to grasp the spongy carcass and place it in the pan and sop up the puddle of grease.

Surely it is her duty to tell Mr. Henry what has happened to his cat. "These people are from a simple agrarian culture," she will tell him. "They are good people. They did not understand what they were doing. They thought they were being thrifty, causing less of a hardship for their sponsors and the town. They acted as they have done before in order to live—by trapping game." But Mr. Henry will not understand. He will be terribly injured by what has happened. The memory of the ugly hulk of the cat's body in the oven keeps passing through her mind. Then she sees it fall sickeningly to the floor. The cat was the old man's only companion. How could he possibly forgive her or the Lieus or anyone for what has happened? It might be more merciful not to tell him. Then he will not have to imagine the horrible sight in the oven. Let him think the cat ran off and died of old age? Was she just being cowardly to think of it this way, just making it easier for herself, or would it, in fact, be more merciful? She imagines Mr. Henry coming again to her front door to inquire about his cat: She says, *I was just this very moment on my way across the street to tell you some very sad news.* Mr. Henry falls heavily to the porch floor and clutches at his heart.

She might tell Jerry about the cat—as a way of helping her decide what to do. He has sometimes joked about the old man walking his cat into their yard whenever they are away, as he does with other neighbors, joked about the grass being killed by catpiss or coming home after a two-week absence to find the house surrounded by piles of cat feces. Jerry will probably find the situation amusing, or it will make him angry. "Now maybe you'll admit that you've made a horrible mistake in bringing them here," he might say. "Now maybe you'll admit for once that you could have been wrong."

Saang

Many women have trouble with soap in their plastic machines at the Laundry-mat, and they squirt medicine into their noses and smile. Soldiers are lying in a ditch beside the road with bleeding arms and feet, and one man is missing from his head. Huge airplanes take off on the runway and fly at the sunset.

Leslie

Leslie has a disturbing dream. She and Saang are out for a walk along the jogging trail. She sees a worried expression on Saang's face that bothers her, affects her mood, even under the surface of her consciousness where time is blown up like the microscopic view of a cell or shrunken as in a computerized aerial-photo of the lunar landscape. She sees Saang walking into a web. She can tell that Saang does not know the web is there, whipping around her ankles. Leslie tries to explain it to her, but her voice is like a distant radio signal, fading in and out. Suddenly, the soil around them is dry and rocky and crawling with long-tailed rats. The rats have yellow eyes and ugly jaws and tongues like giant iguanas. Saang's feet drift an inch above their snapping, lecherous faces.

Leslie wakes up in a sweat. She reaches over to Jerry's side of the bed, but the bed is empty, the sheet cold. The digital clock says 1:58.

She gets up and pulls on her bathrobe and wanders down the hall to Jerry's study. No one there. She checks for a light on elsewhere, tiptoeing barefooted down the cold stairway, feeling her way along the bannister, then, arms outstretched, thin as a ghost in the darkness, reaching for the edges of the woodwork, the edges of the doorframes. But there is nothing but blackness. A car rumbles distantly in the street, and reflected light passes across her face in the shape of a network of warped panes.

She falls asleep again: The asphalt steams in the early morning heat. The road goes on and on, past groves of maples, fields, crossroads, barns with cattle waiting sullenly for release. She passes a farmer's house and strides out into the open country. She is a long way out, perhaps eight miles, cruising steadily on her hot, slick legs. Up ahead, far up the long road, a dark brown pickup turns lazily out of a farmyard and drifts toward her, the profile of its bulbous fenders squaring up with the sloping berm and fence-rows. Then it accelerates furiously, the rounded lenses of its glassy headlights suddenly bearing down on her like the eyes of some gigantic mythical demon.

A dark cloud moves across the face of the sun, and the wind begins to stir the high grass. She is bounding down the center of the road, and the pavement is clear for miles ahead except for the brutal scarred grille of the pickup, sweeping down upon her. She picks up her pace, sprinting now. She glowers at the faded hood, feels the rush of air, and sees, at the last moment, as the grille is actually striking her, that the driver is only her husband Jerry, and Jerry's eyes look down at her and are full of regret.

When he comes in, she is still there in the darkness, doubled over, crying into the couch cushion, which smells faintly moist and acrid, like coats returned from the dry cleaners on a damp day; and then he is above her, leaning into her, patting her shoulder and crooning endearments into her ear that are nothing but lies, she knows, miserable lies, every one of them. How can he fail to realize that she could never, ever, be deceived by such self-serving, transparent lies?

Leslie

She runs and runs, her feet drumming on the asphalt like pistons, like the metal thrusting parts of an oil rig, something mechanical and inexorable and indestructible. Something unremitting. Or another thing: anesthetized, falling, soaring, diving, like a wounded gull, like a lemming rushing to the sea and diving over the cliffwall. Soaring. The heat rises into her face and back, the flush and swelling of the blood, the sweat breaking out, the sense of timelessness and oneness with the earth. The pain and the absence of pain. She stops suddenly and walks, enters a grove of trees beside the road, far from any house or watching eyes. Some force has taken over her body now. It forces her to stop, to lean against this particular small tree, to press herself forward against its thin, hard living surface, while she tenses the muscles in her legs and buttocks and moves her fingers slowly over the tautness of the sapling and of her body. The oaky smell of the bark is a wildness inside and outside herself, an intoxication that carries her mind and breath away.

Leslie

She cannot live in the same house with him any longer, that much is clear. His presence is suffocating, nauseating. The energy required to deal with his presence, or the threat of his presence, with its stench of cigarette fumes and counterfeit pain, leaves her drained and pale and feeble. She has to find somewhere else to go. She realizes she has been thinking for some time that she might like to settle into the small side-porch next to the Lieus on a more permanent basis. She enjoyed the simplicity of the two rooms, the light from the high windows, the promise of comfortable solitude; and the idea of greater proximity to Saang and the Lieu family seems inviting too. A chaste and sensible existence seems possible there, not to mention the additional appealing fact that the place is empty and available. She could be closer to the children to help mold them, to help teach them the language. . . She could substitute at the school to contribute to the upkeep of the family. She gets out the Samsonite and begins packing energetically. The sunlight of a surprisingly balmy February day streams in across the bedspread, and she feels almost happy for the first time in weeks.

Saang

Less-lee brought her suitcases and wishes to move onto the side-porch. She asks if this is okay with me. We sit in the bay window and discuss her upset. The lines near Less-lee's mouth are tight and sharp. Her earnest face is very thin. Less-lee's husband was not a good husband for a woman to have. Poor Less-lee is a miserable woman because of this plight. Less-lee cooks tea and we sit for a long time with the teacups and bread. Then Less-lee holds my face in her two hands and cries and places her head in my lap like a small child. We are trying to think of what to do next, sitting in the sunlight in the afternoon in our small house here in the United States of America.

TWO POEMS

GEORGE EVANS

CWM

Against canyon and skull

the hunter's leather creaks,

insect cracks its death
against flesh & ear—

insouciance
flatters a brain flat—

the room is troubled
with objects.

Last night I last saw B
bending from the porch rail her
breasts swaying watching
traffic. We are done.

Match flares:
angel head searching
through cans
by sulfur curbs

down alley:
beginnings of a face
in a small cage of fingers.

The west:
ocean of rocks,
sewing machines,
ocean of hearts,
coal,
bodies,
silence tossing
its waves at the distance,

dog's blood
rushed in its case,
the bitching lovers
beat one another next door—

clatter of the steel winged train,
bow sprits crack, animals
spring by the moon
into cups on the table and
a conduct the sort of which
earth must come to
rips from the climate—strain:

bottles & tools & watches:
the mechanized bones
begin:

•

So in a household, so in the world:
a lie is a colony—

you can't wind up a house worn down
so plates & spoons dance.

The weak shoe will tear.

I observe you, city, carved by the mind as by wind,

& grow old in unknowable country,

of the dead thinking god
what words might have loved me

& hear a knife growing behind
& want understandings of night not once
but in all lives of the moon

•

Young men wander at night looking for love
& are sobered by love————————————
no center, only terror understood by terror,
the neon too close to mystical parts
for beauty

•

A storm works its way across the floor

:

Snow embraces the stone: peonies
a moment color stops
for nothing—

azaleas, morning
systems, this room

an island, part of the wind
birds cross—

two lives here at once:
one to please/one to fear
to please:

I get up & go then
and stay to go,

leave & never leave:

there's love holds the air
both where it's been & where it needs to be

•

Stars roar computers cars pass electric steam gasoline how
to love sane (wind, solar, atom) how

:

The frontier crosses me

:

It rips your spine loose
like color wire peeled
from telephone line—

bones rise in your mouth,
words build coastlines
on concepts of a sea
without water,

but words
are a steady migration,

a sky spanning the blooms

SATURDAY TOWARDS EVENING

1:

Switches hit low
riding Dodge & Ford

humping, young men
in hairnets,
shirts buttoned to the neck—
girls in black lipstick,
dark purpled cheeks,
eyeliner back to their ears:
Promenade & Spanglish
back, forth, around,
rap sound
bone-deep loud.

2:

The Chat & Chew:
white saucers and coffee,
hamburgers on the grill
like Cadillacs,
waitresses grim so foul a pit
what do, one of them asks,
you want you
son of a bitch?

3:

La Santaneca de la Mission
next to Sophia's Pizza,
glitter and throb, Pioneer
Chicken its windows wide
salt & oil of the sea
biting the air spicing it
Chinese King's Panaderia
its lights on in the back
cleaning up: Mahjong tiles
and Latin music click.

4:

As darkness comes
TV flickers above the bar
in Carlos' Club,
a risen moon,

a lady walks her baby
outside waiting on the sidewalk
jukebox wails
it glitters in smoke
these are good times
where the sun drops
leaving no scar
where it goes.

FIVE POEMS

RICHARD M. BOMSTEIN

:PORTRAIT: "BUTCHER FROM THE ITALIAN
RESTAURANT" (AMERICA, 1983)

"I hear
    you are the **worst**
               offender. ." the butcher shouted
                  as I punched in ". . come
                         right
                   this way—" He'd
                been weighing
                    some meat
                      but now
                        he led
                          me
             to the backroom. .
                 "I'm gonna
             tell you
                this
                  just
              once. ."
                he said
           ". .everybody
                else
         understands. .

so pay attention. .

when

the boss

wants you to

dosomework before leaving. .

you do it. .

capisc

"B

somebody else

had me

do something else. ."

"I'm **told**. ." the butcher replied

". . that you think you're

sospecial. .

but nobody else. .

has that "problem".

"THE INQUEST" (AMERICA, 1983)

He'd "caught" me doing nothing. I was on the opposite side of the
street, with my hands behind my back, when we saw each other.
He was puzzled as he looked at my face. ."What are you **DOING**?"
he shouted across the street "Nothing. ." I slowly answered, recall-
ing that I'd seen him in several places. "Nothing," however, was no
"answer," for he seemed even **more** baffled. "Night off. ." I tried
again, from 20 yards away ". .beautiful night. ." "Where do you
work?" he asked "At a restaurant. ." I replied "What's your **posi-
tion**?" and now the dough had risen, the bread was between us, as
we met by the laundromat "I'm a manager. ." I said, and now his
questions had drawn me into a fixed line: I'd abandoned all quiet
to allow his "inquest" "So **who** do you manage?" he asked ". .are
you a. .**chef**?" "No. ." I said "My name. ." he said ". .is Sam. .
Sammy Byrnes. ." and he pulled his hand out, as I had "earned"
his name, for his inquest was partially over. I shook his hand. .
"Dishwashers. .streetfighters. .**that**'s who I manage. ." I said
"Oh. ." he answered ". .that's. .**important**. .**very** important. ." I

was unconvinced by this response, but was relieved that this
inquest was almost finished. I even asked what **he** was "doing."
"Teaching. ." he said, as his face began shaking ". .but it doesn't. .
help. .when you aren't. .working. . ."

:PORTRAIT: "OLD MAN BY THE BUS STOP" (AMERICA, 1983)

". .aren't you waiting at
   the wrong stop?" he wanted to
   know "No. .I wait
   everywhere. ." I replied. We'd been
   riding the same bus for
   years. "Me **I** ride. ." he said ". .to
   break up the routine. .you know. .ya
   get up. .ya **live** alone. .
   and ya have t'get out. ." "So what
   do you do?" I asked. He laughed, and
   then pointed "I get
   on, ride her that way, and ride her
   back. .and that's that. ." he said. Our
   bus came and we boarded. ". .I have
   an ulcer. ." he said ". .you can ask **anyone**. .
   I almost **died** one time. ." "Were you in
   the hospital?" I asked "**Noo**. ." he answered "not **me**. .but at
   home in my bedroom, I drink
   milk and vodka, and it
   evens me out. .but I
   don't get drunk—"

"THE SPLIT": (AMERICA, 1983)

"He don't buy her the suit
   he'll **never** see her. ." She'd been

talking of her former husband
to the woman next to her in the taxi ". .You think. ." the latter
asked ". .your daughter will get clothes?" "Carl. ." she
answered, ignoring this question ". .has
a **check** coming. .and I'm pregnant. .with twins. .they're
our twins. .and if we didn't need him. .I'd **never** want
him back. ." The taxi moved towards her apartment
complex "Do you really think. ." the adjacent woman
asked ". .that he'll come back?" "**He'll** come back. ." the single
mother said ". .he come over almost every night. .he come into
the hall. .I let him press the button. .I keep him
outside. .and watch him . .and
keep him hanging. . ."

:PORTRAIT: "THE BUSINESSMAN" (AMERICA, 1984)

". .Business relationships are based on trust. ." he said to a lady as
they sat in the coffee shop ". .I'm a businessman. ." he stated
". .let me give you an analogy. .it's a primitive analogy. .it's what
I call the analogy of the "hunter-warrior". .let's say we're in a
forest. .and we see each other for the first time. .we'll attack each
other. .unless there is a **line** between us. .what I call a "line of
trust". ." "Great analogy. ." the lady said. And they both drank
coffee. ". .And that's how it is. ." he reasoned ". .between
management and labor. .the moment that employees lose faith in
management. .**that** is the moment of bad business. ." The lady
listened with her cup in her face ". .I'm a businessman. ." he said
". .and I know about **trust**. .but this has nothing to do with **our**
relationship. ." He stopped speaking, then began again ". .I'm
going downtown. .wanna come with me?" "No. ." the lady said
". .I can't. ." They started towards the door. .The businessman
saw a familiar man, and approached him with great exuberance. .
". .How ya feeling?" he asked. Then he reintroduced himself,
reciting loudly his own name. .". .Tom Morrison. ."

THE CONSOLATIONS OF MATRIMONY

EZRA POUND (writing as Oge Terrence O'Cullough)

Edited by Donald C. Gallup

INTRODUCTION

Ezra Pound's interest in the classic Japanese Noh theater had been stimulated by his work with the notebooks of Ernest Fenollosa, a pioneer historian of Japanese art in the United States. Fenollosa had studied the Noh drama intensively in Japan from 1898 to 1901 and, with the help of Japanese scholars, had prepared outlines and full translations of many of the plays. He died in 1908, and in 1913 and 1915 his widow turned over to Pound her husband's notebooks on Chinese and Japanese literature. Working from those materials, Pound first published *Cathay* (1915)—thus, according to T. S. Eliot, inventing Chinese poetry for our time—and then concentrated on the Japanese drama, doing much of the work while acting as secretary to W. B. Yeats at Stone Cottage in Sussex. Yeats shared Pound's enthusiasm for the Noh plays and contributed an introduction to the first selection of Pound's versions to appear, *Certain Noble Plays of Japan* (1916). Pound's definitive work, *'Noh'; or Accomplishment, a Study of the Classical Stage of Japan,* was published in 1916 in London and in the following year in New York.

Both Pound and Yeats were inspired to write their own plays on the Noh model. Pound wrote his father in February 1916 that these were to be part of a "new new dramatic movement, plays which wont need a stage, and which wont need a thousand people for 150 nights to pay the expences of production." He explained that there would be no compromise, "actors will wear masks, scenery will be mostly imagined, at most a cloth or a screen, and the dominion of [David] Belasco . . . will no longer be coterminous with the known and inhabitable world."

Yeats's first play on the Japanese model, "At the Hawk's Well," was an attempt at a serious Noh equivalent. It was immediately performed with a good deal of success, and Yeats went on to write other plays of similar inspiration. Pound's first two attempts were modeled specifically on the *kyogen,* or comic interlude. The first, entitled "The Protagonist," set in a small Irish hamlet, has as its central characters two policemen taking a prisoner to jail without having been told of the specific charges against him. The comedy arises from their attempts to deal with the questions and theories of curious onlookers.

"The Consolations of Matrimony," the second of Pound's farces, takes place in what is apparently the same village (one character, "Wormy Rooney," is referred to in both plays).

Plans to present "The Protagonist" along with Yeats's play did not materialize, and neither farce nor two other more serious attempts by Pound in the Japanese vein were produced or published in his lifetime. He seems not to have taken the time to make the final revisions that would have resulted in a truly finished version of "The Consolations of Matrimony." The text printed here follows as faithfully as possible his typed drafts in the Collection of American Literature of the Beinecke Rare Book and Manuscript Library at Yale University. Obvious errors and misspellings have been silently corrected and some inconsistencies regularized in order to present a more easily readable text. The play and the quotation from Pound's letter to his father are printed with permission of the Beinecke Library and the Trustees of the Ezra Pound Literary Property Trust.

DONALD C. GALLUP

THE CONSOLATIONS OF MATRIMONY

By Oge Terrence O'Cullough [Ezra Pound]

Dramatis Personae: George Brannan
James Day
A Boy of thirteen with a message

Scene: A room in the cottage of George Brannan, in the village of Ballycurragh, Ireland. Brannan and Day seated at a table.

George: Tim Healan is back from America.

James: I *don't* like him.

George: They have a very free way when they come back from New York and Brooklyn.

James: I don't like him.

George: Ah, Tim's all right. It wakes a man up to go about. Do you think it is much he has with him?

James: I don't care what he's got with him, I don't like the shape of his face.

George: Can't you be civil? Who the hell said you ought to like him?

James: I don't. . . .

George: Ah and come off it. Do you know that rum Rooney?

James: Rooney?

George: Yes, Rooney, Wormy Rooney. Ah, there's a smart fellow, an ornament to the town and a free hand.

James: An *ornament,* with that face! I see nothin' but the small of his back.

George: Now, now, Jimmy, Jimmy, you should have more kindly feelin', more interest as it were, in your *con*temporaries and *co*relationists.

James: What do I care for the lot of them? Can't you change the conversation? You're not always talkin' about foreign people. Here, get a light to your pipe.

George: Well you are civil! What's wrong with you, James, that you talk so snappy? You look downcast.

James: Ah, who wouldn't look downcast? Me, married at my time of life!

George: Is that all your trouble? What age do you think you've got to?

James: Twenty-nine.

George: Two years less than myself.

James: You, you got married last year.

George: And yourself, stole from the cradle. Is it five years?

James: It's seven, and never herself that I wanted. I was stuck on her sister. You know it. A fine figure she had.

George: She had? She *has,* walking the streets of Belfast, her and her figure. Went off with the traveler, is it? A smell of high life. (*James becomes even more gloomy.*) A fine figure, and no sense in her head. You ought, sure you ought to be contented.

James (*groaning, head in his hands*): Ah yes, I am con-ten-ted.

George: And if you wanted the sister, why didn't you take her? Not that you'd have done well. I had no mind to that woman. You're better off as you are.

James: Ah it's all right with you talking. You with the great past behind you. Nine girls you had walkin'. I know you, George Brannan, that used to be out like a tall cat in evening, seekin' your what-you-might-devour. You've been every place in this country. And not with your own name at all times.

George: What's that? What if I have? What are you getting at with it all?

James: What am I getting at, is it? Sure, you strolling, sporting and strolling, and strolling and sporting, and going off nine times to Belfast.

George (*more petulant*): Well what of it? Well! Well!! (*Sharp, jerky speech, very short, "well" like "will."*)

James: Sure haven't you got your mind full of all things, to look back upon?

George: What sort of things?

James: Do you mind now that girl at the mountain?

George (*after a reflective pause*): The one with a little round belly, is it that one you mean? Nannie Keogh?

James: It may be. You said she had a little round. . . .

George: Ah go on with you.

James: And the tinker's wife in the field?

George: I do now.

James: And the girl at the harbour, ah that was a fine girl.

George: A fine girl, a strong girl.

James: Ah.

George: Ah you could have cracked a flea on either one of her breasts.

James: Ah.

George: They're not all like, girls.

James: Ah, what do I know what they're all like at all? Do I know anything?

George: Well you don't know so much.

James: And the one with long yellow hair, with the wild dog in the paddock.

George (*smiles*): She was a fine one.

James: And the girl that time in Belfast.

George: Now it's them city girls.

James: Ah don't I remember? She knew more than you did.

George: Ah she did that. We were going down a lane back of a pub, and she says to me, she did: "You're a mere child in these matters." That's what she said. Ah, it's a powerful lot that a man don't know in a small place.

James: And that was the eighth time you were in Belfast.

George: Ah well.

James: You say right, that a man in a small pale will be a long time filling his head.

George: Well?

James: Well. I don't know much, but do you mind the time in Sleaugh?

George: What a wonderful memory you have for my ways! Sure, you put me in mind of myself.

James: I. . . .

George: Sure I'd clean forgot about the girl in Sleaugh.

James: Don't you know the feel of the whole string of them? How they'd be putting up their face to your face, and. . . . and a pushing against you in the dark? Agh it's a *dull* thing, and *slow* thing to be all the time with *one* woman.

George: Have you been all the time with the one woman?

James: I have.

George: Glory to God! And what were you afore that. . . . ?

and you soft on her sister. . . . that's now gone to the bad. What age were you married?

James: Twenty-two.

George: And a good thing, for you need a strong wife to look after you. My glory to God. (*He laughs.*)

James: What do you do with your laughing? Ain't you now in the same place as I am? One wife all the while.

George: I don't mind. It's not so bad I am. And you too, James Day, haven't you your socks darned, and your tea made, and your floor swept? What's the matter that you are so down?

James: And the girls aren't looking at you any more now, like I used to see them at Chapel. Your time is gone by you, George. Do they now come along talking soft to you?

George: Well now, I don't know.

James: You don't eh? Well I know by the sight of them. And I used to see you among them. You'll not be straying and plucking, straying and plucking. You stay home in the evening, one place all the time.

George: Agh if I do! Amn't I tired of prowling, and going out on wet nights, and going out on cold nights, and getting home in the dawn? Sure I am better now as I am. What have you got so on marriage? Have you no respect for your wife?

James: I've as much respect, as much respect as yourself, that come to yours after twenty-five women, and me pure as a babe.

George: Well if you're so proud of that fact, why don't you walk on into heaven? Why can't you be consistent? Either you envy me or you don't.

James: I don't envy nobody. But I say now as I said, it's a dull thing to be all the time with one woman, and nothing before or behind. Now there's Monahan's widow.

George: Yes, there's Monahan's widow, she's not so tall as your wife.

James: Hasn't she the plans of a new house, of red brick, and never a stroke of work will she do for the rest of her life. It's a fine chance for the lad that she'll take up with.

George: Are you such a slim lad?

James: I'm not bad looking.

George: And what good will that do you? Haven't you got a place of your own?

James: Working and toiling, and no rest and no profit, and always in the same place, and always with the same pay. It's a slow life, and a slow place, and nothing to liven you up from one week to the next week. Have you no power of the imagination, George Moley Brannan?

George: I dare say I can go imaginin' and imaginin' like the next buck in the sow pen, but what's that with Monahan's widow? She's not for me nor for you.

James: Do you think now she'd be wanting a steward at the farm? I think you'd see a lot of the woman if you lived at her farm.

George: Wouldn't she have a solicitor, and she having shares in old Monahan's business in Belfast?

James: Ah there's no advancement for a poor man in a small warty village. Marriage is the end of all things, as me dad said. First ye marry, and then you have children, and then it's one thing and another, you never get up to the top. "Boys," he'd say. . . .

George: Who'd say?

James: Ah me father, ain't I telling you? "Boys," he'd say, "never chew tobacco," and then he'd take another bite off the plug.

George: Agh put away your father and come back to what we were saying. Have you any childeren?

James: Not now but I might have.

George: You've had your wife seven years, that ought to put heart into you.

James: It does not, you never know when you're safe.

George: So you don't approve of Tim Healan?

James: I do not.

George: And you don't approve of the United States of America?

James: Ah what's that to the matter?

George: Where they get a new divorce every week.

James: So I hear. What do they want with that?

George: Well maybe if you didn't go that far, you might at least get rid of your wife. . . .

James: . . . . Eh? . . . .

George: And have a bold shine at an heiress, and give free vent to your powers of imagination. Sure the town's full of orphans.

James: And there's Nelly Casey.

George: Agh, she looking like death without a stitch of petticoat. 'Tis a long way you'd rise in the world with that back to lift ye!

James: And Maggie Nolan.

George: The one with the shape of a barrel, thirty-seven years old, with liver marks on her ear, an orphan. I'd not think of asking for her place at all.

James: Amn't I saying it's nothing at all?

George: Didn't ye say widows and orphans?

James: Well if I did say widows and orphans, I didn't say orphans. I said widows and orphans.

George: And what the hell are you doing with widows and orphans? The parochial board of control is the guardian of the destitute, Jim Day. Widows and orphans!

James: Agh get off your orphans, I'm a sayin'.

George: What are you saying?

James: I'm saying there's no chance of advancement. The same hair on the top of her, the same face, the same bulge on the front of her. The same perverted affection. It is nothing that'll ever happen in the village of Ballycurragh, where there wasn't a horse begat,[1] or a man shaved, or hen went off with the cock of another man's hen yard, or a boar gelded, or a priest drunk, since Adam was three months old. Ah it's a slow place, and a dull place, and no part of the world.

George: It's not always pleasure that comes out of every event, James.

James: Ain't anything better than nothin' at all?

George: It is not.

James: Agh, you're worn out with pleasure. Have you no human feelings?

George: I have so. It's you that's complaining, that can't take a natural enjoyment. What is it now with your wife? She's a neat little piece as any I ever set me hand on.

James: Well, she may be. . . . but. . . . she ain't such a lot. And after you've been seein' a woman. . . . seein' a. . . . Agh I wish I was loose of her. She's like a twist of dough round me neck. She's. . . . Agh I wish to God I. . . .

George: Whist, what are you saying?
Enter a Boy of thirteen.

[1] This reading is doubtful. Pound's typescript has "cow sick," cancelled, with the words in question written above in pencil.

Boy: Is James here? (*He reads from a letter.*) "James Henry Day, E.s.q."

James: What d'you want?

Boy: I saw your wife. . . .

James: I've seen her.

Boy: . . . . and Tim Healan.

James: . . . . Agh.

Boy: They give me this. They were in a side car, on the north hill.

James: The two of them?

Boy: Av course, the two of them.

(*James reads.*)

George: Well, what is it?

James (*reads aloud*): "Dear Mr. Day:

You need not worry. I shall look after your wife, and you needn't bother to hunt for you won't find us.

Your devoted servant,

Timothy Aloysius Healan."

Gimme me hat! Gimme me stick there! Let me get onto him!

George: What's the matter with you?

James: Aren't they gone on me? Get out of me way!

George: Ain't you free of them?

James: Free of them?

George: Ain't you shed of her? Can't you go sparking the widow? Ain't they gone to America, where you get div. . . . ?

James: I'll break in the top of his head! Get out of me. . . . !

George: Ach, won't they be by now on the railroad? (*James exits, George, at the door, shouts after him*): Can't you be sensible? Ain't it like a twist of dough round your neck she was? Ain't it the devil? (*To the boy*): He didn't, now, he didn't have my woman with him?

Boy: He did not.

George: This *is* a bloody slow place.

Curtain.

TWO POEMS

ROBERT GLÜCK

BASHO

			family	as-for	
all	staff-with	leaning	white-hair		
	go	grave-visiting			

		3	2	
1	2	2	2	
	1	4		

It refers to a visit to the family graves in my native village in remembrance of the recent death of my common-law wife. There are present, in addition to myself, my wife's mother, my two older brothers and their wives, and also my wife's brother. (My two daughters are still in Edo.) The "family" is small and certainly made up of elderly people. My oldest brother has no children, and my second brother's oldest son, whom I had adopted, died within the year. I'm already looking forward to my own death and, on this occasion, it seems to me, looking forward to the probable extinction of my whole family as well.

HOKUSAI'S *MANGA*

A samurai tracks through woods watched by the supernatural, which he knows (tiles of carp scale, cormorant feathers for thatch) *but momentarily forgets. Struggles between ancient houses, ridicule, confusion:*

A warrior bragged about his strength; finally he was summoned to a wrestling tournament. He rode through a maple forest of "burning leaves" where he caught a glimpse of an attractive woman dressed in indigo cloth and carrying a bucket of water on her head. The woman was thinking about clumsiness, about a maidservant who dropped one of a set of ten treasured porcelain bowls decorated with long-haired turtles in gold and silver lusters. The master berated her so severely that she jumped into an old well where, from that night, you could hear her hollow voice counting and re-counting the remaining dishes. The warrior dismounted and caught the woman's hand. The woman didn't resist but said dreamily, eyes on the distance, "—or if it rains from a low cloud, or if a shadow half-covers a valley, or a lagoon, or if it doesn't, or if a tree branch looks particularly attractive in itself, surely not because it resembles an elephant's gray leg—"

The warrior sees this as encouragement. He gently takes her arm and the woman releases her hold on the bucket and clamps his wrist under her armpit with such force that a line of cranes whizzes past the couple and nature divides in front of them and rejoins behind. The warrior tries to escape; he digs in his heels and ripples his muscles but he can't pull free, and the woman marches serenely on. The warrior isn't the first who fell in love with a dead person or who misjudges the power of his beloved—or that death should be the basis of her strength. No wonder he's outclassed. We can have no idea of how many ghosts there are or how many people love them; they seem irresistible to a certain type who hungers for excellence.

She's thinking about
revenge, about a cousin who was born ugly because her mother
drowned the cousin's half-sister by an earlier marriage. The cousin
inherited an acre by the river, so a peasant married and then
murdered her. For years she haunted the riverside, driving the
peasant's subsequent wives to their deaths.

Now the warrior pleads
to be set free, says he's due at a wrestling match. The woman
laughs. "I have a little story to tell you. A giant said, 'Nothing can
fell me.' A hero replied, 'A little thing can fell you.' The hero dashed
forward and drove a pick through the giant's little toe. The giant
roared, transmuted pain into rage and scooped up the hero who
said, 'Now I'm going to rent a room at the corner of Hell Street and
I shall be happy to see you whenever you pass by.' The giant tore
him in half the long way and threw both pieces up so high they
disappeared. It was a stunning victory for giants and monsters."

Earlier the warrior felt he had mastered the subject of death. Soon
she will teach him that once you master a subject the subject
masters you. Later the warrior will locate under every smell the
sweet pointed decadence, even though the leaves are on their trees.
Now they embark on a relationship in which every intimacy is
rejected; her bucket will not even spill a drop. The warrior still
doesn't know she's a ghost; if he could glance down he would see
that she has no feet. "You! Wrestling! Live with me for three
weeks—I'll toughen you up!"

UNHEARD OF POEMS BY AUSONIUS CERTAINLY FORGED

THOMAS PARKINSON

Decimus Magnus Ausonius, 309–94, Professor of Rhetoric at Bordeaux, instructed and became friends with Paulinus of Nola (Saint Paulinus) and was tutor of the future Emperor Gratian, who appointed him prefect of Italy and Africa, then, with his son, prefect of Gaul. In 380 Ausonius was made consul. He was in disgrace under the usurper Maximus; Theodosius restored him to favor. He had no political opinions. The greatest wine of Saint Emilion is grown on the estate tradition associates with his name, Chateau Ausone.

The most blatant forgery is the letter to Paulinus, who became a bishop long after the death of Ausonius. The references to Constantine and Julian are ridiculous anachronisms.

Eobracum: York
Burdigala: Bordeaux
Treves: Trier

AUSONIUS TO GRATIAN (AFTER QUELLING THE BRITISH REVOLT)

I write to you from Eboracum,
Three hundred leagues from Rome.
We have put down Crassus.
His head is pickled in this basket.
The Caledonians still prowl the night,
Morale sinks lower with the winter light,
And the troops worship Mithras.
Poignant scent of cannabis.
Paulinus writes to me from Burdigala,
The new wine seems most promising.

The rumors that I hear might be malicious—
You'd still be better off in Rome. Watch Maximus.

AUSONIUS TO PAULINUS (FROM TREVES)

I'm glad that this campaign is almost over.
The climax came this afternoon. My girl
Brought home a great big jug of local wine.
It had a swimming handsome trout in it.
Thus German vintners give their game away.

AUSONIUS REPORTS TO GRATIAN ON A COUNTRY "LIKE A CONQUERED PROVINCE"

Que voulez-vous? Nous faisions l'amour. Eluard.

Their minds are shredded, and their flesh
Gone hateful to them. A bright burst of sun.

What do they do? Make love? They fuck.
Their bodies itch for a prod and lash.

Fine subtleties of love and hate bring passion
To the moment passing. But they are sullen.
What do they do? Make love? They fuck.
They have no style, but lots of nasty fashions.

Their bones will be collected by the power
That turns emotion into bloody funk.
What do they do? Make love? They fuck.
Indifference infests their broken tower.

Once collected they will lie in isolation.
To die, to die—to them it's just a learned pun.
What do they do? Make love? They fuck.
And lie disgusted with each variation.

Our tyrant forces crush their empty lives.
Yet they were shells before, worn-out, undone.
What do they do? Make love? They fuck.
Exterminate them. There's not one I would save.

AUSONIUS IN ROME WALKS IN HIS GARDEN

The plums grow full and fall each day.
The slightest wind will shake them free.
I promenade the garden path
Free from pain, free from wrath.

My children hide beneath the tree
And leap like Indians out at me.
I feign dismay and clutch my heart
To magnify their violent part.

—Tie the white man up, they cry,
For now you must prepare to die.

—O tie me not to the dreadful tree
Where time goes harsh as the sound of the sea.

—Your crimes are great and you must pay
While the red and the bronze and the black go free.

—I only did what the emperor said,
And I can't help you if I am dead.

—You were the emperor's dull tool,
You were the emperor's prize fool.

—You know what you say is a vast untruth,
Show me some love, show me some truth.

—Our filial love for you is great
But can't undo your mortal fate.

—Children, think of your mother's heart
And let your poor old dad depart.

—White man speaks with a forked tongue.
White man tries to deceive the young.
But father, yes, you can go free,
We cut you loose from the ripe plum tree.

AUSONIUS REFLECTS

In my captivity I observed the plums falling
Smashed open from the pressure of their ripeness
While all my losses flashed before my eyes I smiled.
I never laugh or cry in public. Imperial
Gentlemen do not. But when the children
Put me at liberty once more I laughed with them
Forgotten my imperial dignity when I was plum and child
Again and not the emperor's pompous emissary
Grateful to be the butt of savage rites.

Flesh falling, there is nothing so complete as plums.
I must reclaim that German girl at Treves—proconsul
Antonius has no real use for her, his long-nosed wife
Poking through unused rooms to crush all delicacies
That might appeal to his thwarted palate. A letter
Should in thirty days recall her to my side
And leave his wife with far less cause to prowl.

Rivers and vineyards, plum trees and girls. Politics.

AUSONIUS AS POLITICIAN TO ANTONIUS (ROME TO TREVES)

Gratian is pleased that you have pacified
Those fierce and restless tribes that threaten life
Within his justly settled territories.
The peace of Rome be with you and your wife.
My memories of Treves are so deep with me
I'd like some fixed reminder of those times.
The little German Girl I left with you
Could join the first returning caravan.
Her voice and lute are pleasing to my ears—
Give her this song to practice on the way.

AUSONIUS TO PAULINUS, ON RECEIVING HIS LATEST MANUSCRIPT

Remember those days and nights—I remember
Those girls laughing, laughing, no one could begin
To stop. With what effort. And then resumed.

Laughter, laughter, and nights like one vast
Star so no one of us knew the time, it was always
Early, skulking home you and I padding in like cats.
Poems too, revelations, irritations, forgiveness.

One immense clarifying light. Abandons of poetry,
Girls, liquor, food, talk. Sometimes
All the rest seemed only a way for us to stay
Together within a world not always welcoming
Either one of us—these are our days,
And they are passing, teeth dwindling,
But we've been lucky in our wives and other
Necessities. Lonely, moving toward what
Comes next, and happy in that, I pause
In this springlike November, remembering
All that brings me here, you early in my thought.

Friendships of poets are never simple. Ours
Has a bond past death.

AUSONIUS TO PAULINUS FROM TOMI (THRACIA)

Paulinus, I can hear your voice, your lute
Tuning. Birds here are scarce—too many cats.
If I express my loneliness, these brutes
Here reinforce it. Evenings, I sit
Upon the terrace that commands the sea
And read state documents. That news is bad,
No worse than what you hear. We are crumbling.
The empire's dying, dead. I take to bed.
And cannot sleep or say my prayers. I see
Desolation and decrepitude.

I cling to friendship. Barbarian blood
Stains the waters of the estuary.
Our troops have won another victory.
Our general was ecstatic over dinner
And said, Ausonius, we are winning.
That statement was for Gratian's ears, not mine.
I'd seen the famous victory with my eyes.
I smiled and told him that was very nice.

Paulinus, he had conquered sticks and stones
And filled the field with women's and children's bones.
Tomorrow night they'll devastate his camp.
I leave tomorrow afternoon for France.

AUSONIUS TO GRATIAN FROM BURDIGALA

Imperial friend, I'm writing to resign.
Prefect, consul, I've been those two, and more.
And all through your affectionate piety.
More than an emperor, more than a son,
You have the right to keep me from my ease,
But do not exercise it. I've gone dry.
The nights lack length to let me rest. The days
Are shorter than my work. Let me return
To poetry and wine. Do not keep me
From my aging pleasures. Burdigala
Calls me, city of my birth, and my death.

AUSONIUS IN BURDIGALA TO PAULINUS
IN SANTIAGO

You chide me in my great age, Paulinus,
Because I keep a mistress and enjoy my wine
Without a daily meditation on the blood
Of your strange weak and mortal human god.
Ausonius, you write in loyal horror,
How could you?
                It's not as easy as it was,
I do concede, I'm much more conscious
Of my pumping blood that merely used to flow.
My wife informs me that I grow quite red
With wine and exercise. I'll cut out gardening.

I'm shortening my life. You say as much
But what's that matter if my soul is saved?
You say your god will rescue all the sinners
At any time. That seems capricious to my stoic
Eyes but subject to a favorable sense.
As I lie dying from my earthly pleasures,
I'll trust your word and abdicate my soul
To all ascetic virtues and express regret
That I've been so immoderate in my senses.
But you don't really care about my life.
The soul's your great concern, and most of all
Your own.
        I tried those prayers you taught me—
The empire crumbled, Gratian became a kook
And ran around Paris in Scythian clothes
Until he stuck his neck (smack) under Maximus' sword.
Your prayers were no more help than common sense.

You say I drink too much. Well, damn it, man,
I'm lonely. You're the one that shortens my life,
Thinking of you out on the northern tip
Of that peninsula with those savage Celts
(I'm sure they're Celts, malign and dirty).
You were the only decent poet in the Empire,
So you left me here to drink away the days
With no decent literate conversation.
Let all religions go to hell for all of me,
They just encourage gloomy self-indulgence.

My thought is cheerful. O, I've tried. I thought
And thought about those bloody wounds—what use?
My own conclusion was that only fools
Could like a world run by a God so cruel
He'd let his own son suffer for mankind.
It hurts me that you suffer for the cruel.
Cruel men, a cruel god, that's all
I see encouraged. At least Lucretius
Had no tolerance for the pain inflicting
World Augustus gave us for stability.

Stable. All he did was fashion a design
For making life so painful men would take
A kind of stupor for reality.
That's not for me, stupor or cruelty.
You say that I gave up the life of spirit
To know a world of power. Yes. To know
A world. Poets have no other business.
Spirit, power, it's up to us to know them
But not to serve. The services I rendered Gratian
Were simply to report what eyes could see.
Influence was not in it except what favors
I could do my friends, like you. It was I,
And the greater fool for doing it, that gave
You land in far Galicia. I—Consul Ausonius—
Used my mighty powers to send to Christian exile
The only man with any sense of prosody.

In time you'll have your Christian emperor.
There was a man called Constantine in Britain
Who had the proper smell of unctuous piety.
In time I'll have my pagan resurrection.
They'll call my emperor apostate, yes,
Too civilized to suit their cruelty.
"A prophet?" you inquire, with your engaging laugh,
"Ausonius, you grow soft. Stick with poetry."
Yes, I'll stick with it and stick the world
With one poor remnant of the grand tradition.
But only poor because I had no friend
To tell me when the line had lost its life.

AUSONIUS RETIRES ALTOGETHER, REFUSING APPOINTMENT FROM THEODOSIUS

I have celebrated sixteen cities, written sincere
Panegyrics to the Emperor Gratian,
Even counted all the fish in that boring Moselle.

I presided over Italy, Africa, and France.
Filial piety attended all my days. My father
Saw my success. My son has taken over my prefecture.
My wife from childhood doesn't even mind my
Twenty-year-old German slave girl. There is
No literary form I don't know and master. This soil
Does something special to grapes. I have the best
Table and bed in France.

                             Of course something's missing.
You're right to say I can't be satisfied.

I had only two students worth remembering:
Gratian dead; Paulinus lost to the forms of things
With the savage Iberians and his crozier.
One Emperor who betrayed Rome's customs;
One Bishop who takes me away from the easy gods.
There must be something wrong with education.

BEDS

MARTIN BAX

> *"Half our days we pass in the shadow of earth; and the brother of death exacteth a third part of our lives. A good part of our sleep is peered out with vision and fantastical objects, werein we are confessedly deceived!"*—
> Sir Thomas Browne

One Sunday morning after the war, I was lying in my bed when I heard my father shuffle across the landing into the bathroom which lay just behind my bedhead. Before he turned on the water (so did he mean me to hear?) he muttered, "Bloody Bitch—gone to church—and taken the car with her." Unfair, unfair, how could she have got to church—a good five miles away—without the car. But as I lay there I knew that this was no comment on my mother's churchgoing or on her early rising but rather on her not lying down—beside him—in a bed.

It was many years since it had been established that my parents had separate bedrooms: it went back to days before the war when we lived in quite a different house and where my parents had that big room with its own bathroom and those big twin beds pushed together. But then also, across that landing, they had, or rather my father had his "dressing room." Some mornings I remembered seeing him shuffle over there. They were Victorian born, were both my parents, so that room in itself was not surprising in a middle-class house—only the use it was put to.

I had graduated (this again way back before the war) to my

own adult bed and separate bedroom. There I lay then in what seemed a huge bed which you could crawl into and totally disappear. I awoke one hot summer night to find I had disappeared in this way and lay buried, sweating, half suffocated and a bit panicked till I pushed my way out beyond the bed and out of my bedroom and into the passage—not crying but making enough noise to rouse my unsleeping father who emerged—this in the middle of the night—not from the bedroom but from the dressing room.

"I got stuck in my bed," I said.

"It's the middle of the night," he replied and took me back and, no doubt, put me back into my own bed.

I was sufficiently curious in the morning to ask my mother—my father long gone to work—why he was banished to that (very high, I remember) bed in his dressing room. My mother, startled, made some reply:

"Oh, my snoring"—she did snore—"keeps him awake." But even then at the age of five or six I knew that the noises of the night do not flush a lover from his bed. Thence to the next house where two beds were still kept in one room but one of them, I fear, was never used and then the move to a final home where there were those two clear separate bedrooms each with its single bed.

But with the war my father sent me to safety. I would have preferred of course to stay, having no fear of wars, but plenty of strangers, strange rooms and strange beds. I was away then to the single iron-framed beds favored by the poorer sorts of boarding schools. There were people, of course, who would share them with you.

"I say, Ursula," begged her chum Lesley, "may I come into your bed, so that we can talk without disturbing the others!" And talk they did—Suddenly Lesley's strong impulsive arms were wound tightly round her and Lesley's voice with a break in it exclaimed: "Don't be such a dear idiot! Of course you're wanted especially by me." These friendly schoolgirl beds are not like the ones I encountered. Although we crossed indeed from one bed to another and when we lay in rows with partitions between the beds, hands, strong young male hands, would force their way under the partition to reach out strongly for one's body, one's flesh. I reached back from my single bed yearning for something more than sleep; not blaming but wondering if, in dismissing me, my father had wanted me to experience the nature of separation.

Alone, I have spent many years in beds—single beds—and have slept alone in double beds, even in king-sized beds. Single beds, beyond those cold iron ones, include bunk beds, bean-bag beds, couchettes, air mattresses, sofas—my feet in a chair, and the places one has lain which don't really justify the name bed, viz. a mat on a concrete floor of a school in Heraklion. South African prisoners (so Breytenbach tells us) call this "sleeping camel" because the skin on the hips eventually becomes calloused. Helen Suzman may have been responsible for getting these wretched prisoners beds and the prisoners referred to her as Auntie, but in a way she was and is more of a father to them.

There have been beds, too, which I have slept in, which themselves have made some attempt to provide you with something more than sleep. Like the bed in the Chicago motel which when fed a quarter would shake and rattle like a washing machine so you awoke tossed and spun. Or beds accidentally shared with friends who had not purposed to share the night together. Peter and Edwin each lay sleepless on the outer sides of their beds for fear they might touch, but Tony when I shared with him (used no doubt to sharing on Cheetham Hill) lay untroubled beside me. I lay rigid, sleepless, till dozing at last I was awoken by his movement and tensed again as he rose up beside me, slid open the window above my head, and peed out of it into the night. Alone I *prefer* the narrow beds like that which Wellington campaigned in, which as a lady commented to the great man was so slender one could not twist in it.

"When it's time to turn over, it's time to turn out."

To the days then (which I think my father sought) when the beds I slept in were shared. The rushed hopes of youth when we lay on a bed so narrow that I slept with an arm propped on the ground to stop me falling out while you lay compressed against the wall. And the secret beds we have shared; that night when we entered the wrong room and I hid behind the door while you encountered the ancient lady who told you of the shape and state of her heart.

And there have been those occasions when seeking a shared bed, at the penultimate hour one has been dismissed with a "I'm sorry love, but I can't make love in snatched hours in a narrow bed."

That sort of dismissal leaves one creeping out into the night forced to trace a path through dim corridors, past stiff fire doors to a narrow room with again a narrow bed on which one is forced to lie without the succor of love or friendship.

(One could here, in parenthesis, talk of other beds. Beds of Alabaster, Beds of Agate, Beds of Antimony. All the rare beds. Or again perhaps the more mundane beds—asparagus beds, watercress beds (down by the riverside), once a whole bed of radishes. My father liked these vegetable beds well enough, would even work at them a little, but liked best to clean them out and burn their waste on a slow fire he tended all day. Forgetting botanical beds we could together view the bed on which an ancient printer will lay his lead to set up the text of this tale.

And then there is the issue of historical beds. I have already animadverted on the beds of the Good King Rene of Provence who if one believes history even lay chastely beside the Maid of Orleans. Or I could invoke the famed lover's beds and record how the gods abandoned Anthony there—At midnight, when suddenly you hear an invisible procession going by with exquisite music, voices, don't mourn your luck that's failing now, . . . Or I could even record something in song: "By night on my bed I sought him whom my soul loveth.")

There have been solidly purchased beds—double beds, not those wooden twins my father must have ordered from somewhere like the army and navy stores around 1930 but first a cheap wrought-iron model with a flock mattress. It stood square but not firm, the mattress molded itself into lumps and the soft metal legs slowly sprayed out and slowly from the heights we were lowered to the ground.

Those beds which do duty in the day as couches we seemed to collect. The first was an unwanted gift, a subsidiary part slid out from under the main springs and a doubled-out mattress attempted to correct the difference in height between the two sections, but it failed and we lay on two platforms one above the other arguing the night away as to who was the superior. That all might be described as pillow talk. But when my father came to stay it was the bed on which he—alone of course—was accommodated.

There is the noise of beds—unique to the bed and not to its occupants. One drummed its headboard against the wall and to stop its deathly rattle and to prevent it boring a hole in the wall it was eventually covered with layers of cloth. Those beds made with curiously coiled springs spoke a language of their own, twisting their way into your conscience and your conversation. There was a great continental bed that spoke in the middle of the night like a big bass drum as a board snapped and we were once more deposited on the ground. There were melodious beds and there were mournful beds, there were beds which spoke with a sound of menace.

You could try moving the beds around. I noticed you doing this. Changing lovers you moved your bed. It used to stand just inside the door so you could rush in and flop on it and grab some instant sleep. Although as you said you needed your sleep you changed its position and hid it behind the door. It became a Surreptitious Bed which one could slink onto unobserved and without, you said, making the slightest change in one's life style. It was just somewhere to hole out until the weather changed. You could go further and actually move the beds from one room to another, changing the purpose of the rooms and the purpose of the beds.

All the time you could say the beds were getting harder. There was indeed the hard-up bed bought at an Oxfam shop but it had a twisted spring and had to go in the end like all the others. So it was time to go for something that made no attempt to massage the limbs or assuage the spirit. It was not a bed to sink into but rather something on which the surgeon could operate. It was a bed that certainly gave nothing to you but rather took what it could. Still it was a bed on which two could lie—at a pinch.

All this time while I speculated in beds, my father was getting older. Did he speculate or conceive of all the uses there were to a bed? To be sure he was still a light sleeper: something disturbed him in the night—maybe he was up still searching for an errant son. He would rise, don a few clothes, and then begin to tramp round the house. When one roused oneself and came to him, he would accept that it was the night, return to his bedroom, strip off the old cardigan he had put on over his night clothes, and seemed to settle himself peacefully enough for sleep again. But if one lay down oneself one would be disturbed in five minutes when he rose again to pursue his nightly marching. It was easier in the end to leave him circling the house than to try and explain to him the real purposes of the night.

My friend Taner took a personal interest in these nocturnal wanderings of my father and saw in them a desire to be back in the drudgery of his working days in an office. It was true he saw them as nothing else but drudge but Taner believed that nevertheless he missed his years of commuting on slow trains and that he woke to his Bradshaw and began to dress for a past journey. It was a possible explanation but I doubt myself if that was what the old man was really looking for on those nocturnal ramblings.

Came the night, came the day when he rose no longer from his bed but lay washed up beyond the tides which had carried him to and fro for so many years. The doctor called daily, not attempting too strenuously to oppose the course of these events, but merely to ease them with some minor remedies.

"Why don't you," he said to mother, "offer him a little brandy?" This she did, choosing to give him the little sips he was prepared to take not from a glass but from an egg-cup—perhaps there was some obscure symbolism in that. My father had always been proud of his ability to speak French and liked to borrow phrases from that language but even I was startled when on one of those latter days he replied to a kindly inquiry about his well-being from the doctor with the phrase "Comme ci, comme ça." He turned his head a little restlessly but then stilled and closed his eyes on us. He seemed at last to lie there at rest knowing that there was a need for sleep.

NEAR THE PACIFIC, EARTH DREAMS

EDWIN HONIG

1   The Dream of Earth Passing

Here bedded in old time
near the Pacific
the sea loses
its lulling allurement
rising to hurl and destroy

Poseidon
son of Kronos
once given ocean
his castle of chaos
guarded
by sea monsters' teeth
his trident—
faithless untamed
and unhappy enough
to swallow the earth
rocked himself
swelling
tide upon tide
smashing the land
to snatch back
the shapes of all life
that had climbed ashore

Now out of seas' grasp
in high mountain
comes the ancient
new dream
of all earth's passing

How again
there could be
no sky
and no window
no wall
and no house
the garden ash heaps
the park a grave
music silent
in the yearning ear
and sitting in a chair
or lying underground
have no name

How to the last
dim call
eyes turn drowning
in the old beyondness
space no longer covers
and the long light
blackens shut

How nothing
rolls or whispers
but a hole
vanishing
with nothing going in
but the color
of would-be speed
in attitudes
of daylight going
and creatures sunk
in dumb motion

about to emerge
as if roaring
what no one hears

Except if time
were believed again
and everything told
written again
and from sleep
a loosening smile
answered
what once had been
set and geared
awakening a tear

Then words
breaking silence
would start again
waves recall boats
to crossings
uphold us again
and the watched light
masterfully fly
to its shadows
lumbering off
with all life could be
told and untold

2   Touching the Seed

Once earth was heard
touching the seed
to scatter them all

Quick with purpose
she came
The others came later
by chance—hurricanes

trade winds
volcanoes—
hurling seeds farther
and farther from home

Few blossomed in season
Most froze and died
Some picking up
to plant themselves
sideways in niches
spread among driveways
walls of ruined towers
sprouted there
stunted and cold

Smothered
by insects and fungi
some wilted
ground in the dust
Tornadoes
swept away houses

Some seeds perished
in bathrooms
some after rabbits
ate them
some after raccoons

Then
a few moping birds landed
and seeds found themselves
living in tundras
so far from nowhere
it seemed like the moon

So they multiplied
blown everywhere
into the planets
and stars

3   Heart Beats in Silent Mountain

Close to
his country of mind
he'd find himself waiting
there on a bend
in the mountain
some late spring afternoon
poised in half shadow
neither bobcat nor boulder

A presence stuck there
he'd find himself
fathering
almost the son
of himself

He'd recall how the water
dangling behind
kept trickling
till it hung endless
still falling
through soggy thick moss
escaping

There
where deer drank
he'd spy in the mire
footprints
matching his own
and a leonine passing
from sunlight to shadow
fastening onto him

Is it that I alone
feel it?
—then again
Whoever you are

must finally be
what you feel

All he found in his mind
had slipped by him
time after time before—
like someone
who liked country dances
rolling intricately
with him
he'd whip by smiling
with self and partner
interreflected
as heart dully asked

Why can't I love
beyond dancing
the dancer mother
daughter or wife
in body beloved
who if not mine
might be a part of me
glimpsed in another?

Why can't my heart
before bowing out
deflecting
the bestial downgoing
sniff out some reason
for losing itself?

In earthy unreason
the mountain kept still
grown centuries tighter
with encumbered trees
he thought were listening
when two jays screamed
and went fleeing a shadow—
their own

Past him he saw
one feather rise
not touching ground
seeking the body
that shed it

The blue feather
that rose
dropped again
to lie grounded
and bent

Day deepened
water went purple
with heart's blood
to make more of the mud
stuck to his boot
The mountain
defied further telling

He lounged in the skin
of his presence
with boulder and tree
grown far beyond him—
afterthoughts
buried under his foot

What can I utter
to give this time
new word or old—
anything not
already told?

4   The Dream of Earth Returning

Earth at its lowliest
that stood up

towering over him
would one day answer

Earth underfoot
descending lower than oceans
whose glinting lit eyes

Earth twisting the light
and turning his eye
into a figure
of self abounding
was telling

Where wind is detained
time is appeased
makes no notable furrow
eases the heart

Where wastes of sky wash
on tender shoots
treelets have burst
hummocks of sod
and we arrive
to infilter each shoot
with parents above us
dead hanging leaves
not yet in the sod

Once
along roadsides
implanted columns
embodied the power
to act to make
fertile

There
women lay
rubbing their bellies

on stone
to have children

Others
buried a sick child
in earth
planted seed over it
to grow with the plant

Where plenty is found
there it is lost
Before nurture swells it
earth dies in a seed

From his niche now
he caught
how the vigil was started
how landfall
hunter and quake
cleared mountains
till cattle and sheep
made pasture

How sunken
the bodies of goddesses
mingling and moistening
in daylight
still turn and glisten
where in broad shade
pass bobcat and cougar
sliding
through shadow and light

Heaped in these quick
sharpened hills
lulled in these round
gradual hills
stretched in these long

plunging hills
lie the earth goddesses

One
headless supine
with belly and breasts
flung open
exposes pubis and bush
thighs ending
deep in her haunches
where from the slope
of her back
another tilts up
high buttocks—
two women of earth
who wait to continue
the vigil of earth

Like a long tongue of flame
a hymn
from Broch's *Virgil*
startles the mind

> *Greater than earth*
> *is light*
> *Greater than man*
> *is earth*
> *and his existence*
> *is nothing*
> *till he breathes*
> *his native element*
> *returning to earth*
> *through earth returning*
> *to light*
> *an earth being*
> *receiving the light*
> *on earth*
> *received in turn*
> *by the light*

and only through earth
earth changing to light

It is now
under the shapening boughs
of a redwood a mountain
lion more sudden than fire
appears
in the clearing
looks back once to gaze
where he stands
stiller than death
then turning and breaking
melts in the thickets

THE HIT

CATHERINE PETROSKI

The long thin nose, the heavy brows, the shock of white frizzed hair standing on end like Beckett's—Yves Roland's is the kind of profile that is easy to caricature. It has been several times already, but then a filmmaker such as Yves Roland is a likely target. In the receiving line he turns a smile to the next well-wisher. His teeth are very small.

"No doubt about it—you're the hit of the festival, Monsieur Roland," the woman next in line says to him. Her *monsieur* is passable, the *r* actually quite good. "What a fabulous talk," she continues. "We're so lucky to have you here."

The woman saying all this to Roland appears to be somewhat fabulous herself: thin, very tall, and dark, in a black silk dress and an immense black straw hat. The kind of woman who looks as though one could never know everything about her. Hers is the only hat in the room, and Roland catches himself thinking what he would make of a detail like that on film. Along one side of the hat's crown lies a huge rose, pale pink, silk, that quivers as the woman speaks. Despite the woman's ease something in her eyes appears literally stunned. Was it Roland's talk? Had someone perhaps tricked her into the lecture hall and hit her with a small deadly mallet between the eyes?

The actual facts of tonight's lecture may have been something of an embarrassment to Festival administrators. More than the usual one or two odd ducks rose and left as Roland spoke. Had a crowd wandered into the auditorium by mistake, or on the wrong night? Or had it been Yves Roland's departure from the announced topic ("The Making of *Le Déluge*"), choosing instead to postulate the influence of the Occupation on French filmmakers of the seventies and eighties. The woman in the rose hat moves to take her leave, to make way for the next to shake his hand, and Roland seizes her hand, shaking it again, finally raising it to his lips. He is all charm. The woman is shaken. Shalimar fills the air thick and sweet, like too much blood.

Yves Roland turns then: full-face to the next person, another woman, totally different. Her face is flushed (or is it that false blush make-up?), her voice is expectant (or is it deliberately breathless?), and she tells him she has been waiting for this moment for a long time. Ridiculous, he tells himself. He has seen this woman a hundred times. No, easily a thousand. Yet, not exactly. If he studies her, he will see how she is different.

Pictures in magazines didn't do him justice, nor did the TV. Everyone agreed to this. Always hidden minicams were catching Yves Roland fleeing, one hand up as if to shield himself from the blow he imagined coming. He would swear at cameramen in French. News editors seldom edited his profanities out. Roland was never sure whether they didn't know what he was saying, or did.

"Tell me what would bring you to a place like this?" the breathless woman asks him. He looks relieved that she is filling the silence. Maybe she doesn't like it here either.

"Money. Nothing more, nothing less."

"Oh, I can't believe that."

"It's true," he shrugs, smiles, turns his pants pockets inside out like Marcel Marceau. "See?" It is a practiced gesture, charming.

She laughs.

"And what brings you here?"

"My husband. Past tense. My ex-husband, now."

"Ah."

"And would anything keep you here, or make you come back?"

"A beautiful woman," he says. It is an answer that comes easily. Roland has always found that to be a superb answer, useful for a variety of questions. And her question was flirtatious enough. His face is perfectly still, except for the insides of his eyes.

"To each his own," she says. She laughs again, and he laughs.

"Let me get you some food, something to drink," he says.

"Oh, please, allow me." She does a Charlie Chaplin après-vous, and he does a Charlie Chaplin après-vous, and they trade several more until the whole room is looking. Then they laugh together, at the room, laughing at them.

"Tell me your name," he says to Clea.

". . . Monsieur Yves Roland." The Fête Cinematique greeted his introduction with the usual tumultuous applause. Another full house. The lighting tonight was too dramatic, but that too was the usual state. The details of Roland's days were, in a fashion, becoming frighteningly similar. Gone, it seemed, was the excitement of not knowing whether a film he wanted to do would be made, or whether the critics would like it, or if anyone would come to see it. After *Le Déluge*, Yves Roland could count on an audience no matter what he did, no matter what the critics said. Another blockbuster was another matter. But those aberrations depended on other things—timing, promotion—and not on the film.

Besides, of all that he had had his share, enough for two careers, and how much could one really enjoy? All that mattered now was work, which had become in recent years a serene and predictable mistress, like a lifetime mate. She could be depended on to lead him into those timeless chutes that took him out of real life into he knew not where. As long as those happened, he had no worry. So what if his young, passionate style had given way to something more considered. Continuity made up for the wild-eyed manner. There was no longer a question about being permitted to do what he wanted to do. He did it, and he was good at it.

Ah, *Le Déluge*, Roland's blessing and his curse. *Le Déluge* was ancient history. Yet always people asked the same questions, always about it. Had people stopped going to movies ten years ago? Refusing to answer, however, would be supremely ungracious. Perhaps the real price of success was always having to answer the same questions. Roland's answers were ready.

A: No, he did not anticipate doing a sequel to *Le Déluge*.

A: No, it was not true that he had found Monique Étoille in a Marseilles brothel, and no, he had not cast her as the lead in *IO*.

A: No, he had no immediate plans to become an American citizen.

A: No, Bergman and he were not bitter enemies. He hardly knew the man—did anyone?

A: Yes, he had children. Three. Nearly grown now. Nothing about them, please.

A: Yes, he had remarried. No, not at the moment.

A: No, he did not find it possible to work to one's fullest extent as an artist and be a marriage partner.

A: No, he was not antagonistic to gays.

A: No, he was not pro-gay. He believed that all people finally do what they must.

I am sorry, he would say then, I must catch a plane.

"And I came to the realization," she was saying, "that I was nothing better than a kept woman."

Roland gives Clea a professional scan. Blond and blue-eyed, all-American, the type always cast as the cheerleader, the girl next door, the eternal ingénue until she can no longer do close-ups even with the soft focus that everyone knows the reason for. In real life this Clea's smile is fine. For the big screen, her teeth would have to be capped. Oh, the kept-woman thing again. "You were married how long?"

"Fourteen years. God, forever. He was a lawyer," she says. "Considering, he treated me very well in the divorce." She looks at him, Kansas and milkshakes and football Saturdays. He nods and notices Clea's stubby hands, nails bitten to the quick. "Not that I ever gave him reason to do otherwise. You know how lawyers are, though."

He knew. "But surely you are being too hard on yourself."

"Well, what else can you call it? He paid my bills, we went to bed. We stopped loving each other long before we stopped making love. Writing became my life." Clea's pink color intensified.

"Ah, you are a writer! I knew, I sensed that you were involved in something creative. So, what did your husband think of your writing?"

" 'That shit ruined our marriage'—that's what he said to me. Maybe it did."

"And what sort of writing do you do? Poetry? Stories?"

Clea's screenplay is about a man (a lawyer), well-regarded in his community, who is addicted to several controlled substances, which her treatment does not specify. Ritually, the man drives about in a fur-lined van in a drugged condition each night between the hours of 2 and 5 A.M. To what end is never exactly clear. Yves can't see an audience ever buying this, but he smiles and nods as Clea tells him. Maybe all will become obvious later. One learns to grant writers certain latitude in getting exposition out of the way. Matters of emphasis, theme, can be handled later with the special economy of film—a gesture, a series of images, nuances of expression, some central detail in the set. What else is a director for?

One night the addict backs out of his garage and accidentally runs over both his wife and her mother, who (innocent of any knowledge of the man's nocturnal habits) have spread their Orvis sleeping bags on the warm concrete driveway in order to observe the Perseid. Despite his altered state, the lawyer realizes the gravity of his situation. He cannot deal with it. He rushes to his dealer, who perceives the man's desperation. The price of whatever it is skyrockets.

When Clea pauses, Roland asks her, "Have you ever tried coke?"

"No," she says. "I smoked some marijuana once years ago. Bill tried it too. Where would you get cocaine in a town like this? I wouldn't even know where to start."

Yves Roland knows it could be done, but sees that Clea thinks he wants her to get some for him. "You misunderstand me," he says, "but the point is, your play . . ."

"Oh, it's *just* a story," she says. Pairs of dimples.

He smiles.

Clea continues outlining the plot, but Roland doesn't listen. He doesn't want to know if her husband was right.

Around Yves Roland the words ebb and flow like a tide littered with so many broken shells and worn bits of old colored glass. It is part of the terra incognita he must face when he accepts these speaking engagements: the after-speech reception. Yves Roland thinks of how a wide-angle camera mounted on the ceiling would capture the advances and retreats of persons and groups. Water seeking higher ground. The crowd's eyes track him like those of lunatics enthralled by their moon, or like the faces of heliotropes following an afternoon sun. At the edge the woman in the rose-decked hat observes him, distanced and formal, like a tree-rose in a palace garden.

Then Roland knows: the rose hat is simply his first wife exactly, though if the two women were put side by side, nine people out of ten would not see the slightest resemblance. No, you have to have lived with a woman like that to know, a woman like Elli and like this woman in the rose hat. It is something Yves can't explain, and could never put on film. It is scent of pasture, like that of dairy cows, and their demeanor of passive resistance. The thought of Elli always makes Roland uncomfortable: Elli, who knew him too well, in ways he wasn't anymore. She refused to understand him, and he couldn't understand her. He needed his freedom. He was tired of her. Perhaps she was tired of him. There had been as many reasons to split as they had time to think up. Maybe, Roland thinks, everyone grows tired of his partner, only some conceal their boredom better than others. He yawns.

The festival chairman checks his watch. M. Roland's time's not up; another twenty-five minutes. And after all, his fee had in their eyes been a fortune.

Suddenly he wants the woman in the rose hat.

It is mad. The backs of his legs tell him to grab her, to tear her expensive dress, to carry her away he knew not where. He knows it is not the kind of thing she is used to. What has happened? It is altogether too absurd. The issue here is one of control and lack of control. Over self, over others, it doesn't matter. Roland wants to pull her hat from her head, wind his fingers in her hair, consume her, lose himself.

He yawns, stretches, faking boredom. Très fatigué, pardon, jet lag. He feels something at his elbow. It is Clea, a glass of wine, a cube of watermelon on a ruffled toothpick, and a second idea for a film. He takes the wine, sights her through the glass's rim.

"Where are your children?" he asks.

"Tim's with bill. Missy's at camp." Clea lowers her eyes. Then she sees and looks up quickly. "Why?"

Oh, she knows. "Haven't you had enough of this party?" he asks. "Wouldn't you like to go somewhere quiet? Sri Lanka, the Hebrides, Bora Bora? You name it."

She laughs and then looks around. The crowd is staying. Many here know her, know her husband. She has stopped smiling.

Can he tell what she is thinking? Yves Roland, think of it. Perhaps she recalls the revolutionary love scenes of his films, the arranged views of passion lighted artfully, draped with swaths of sheet, buttressed by mounds of pillows. Perfection. Shoulders, backs, legs, breasts, kisses, caresses, ecstasy, soft focus, low light. A dream come true.

"Well, O.K.," she says.

It will be a simple matter: these things are always simple matters. They won't go anywhere, really. Her house, his room. Yves reaches for Clea's hand, heading for the door.

Near the door the woman in the rose hat stands facing the other way, talking to the festival chairman, a bespectacled and intense young professor. As Roland passes her, he seems to trip, go off balance, but in fact he has calculated his misstep. He throws a block into the woman's elegant black silk back. She says "Oh!" and lurches forward, her hat jarred from its place and her wine spilling onto the chairman.

The chairman mutters through his teeth, "What a clumsy bastard." He is disgusted. Yves Roland isn't holding up his end of the deal.

Yves continues toward the door, reaching for Clea's hand, as though it is a magnet pulling him against his wishes.

"Mr. Roland," the chairman says, "it's early."

"I'm sorry, I never learn about red wine. Dreadful headache," he lies, stepping backward toward Clea. Yves is now in the hall. Clea is ahead of him, he is still reaching for her hand, practically running. It is as though they are in a silent high boxwood maze. Sound is irrelevant. All that matters is movement, action, and what lies directly ahead.

The chairman leans out the door. "Your envelope—" he says, waving as though he's flagging a train.

"You can mail me the check," Yves calls back to him. Whether they do or not makes no difference. It is, after all, only money.

EIGHT POEMS

DELMORE SCHWARTZ

Edited by Robert Phillips

THE DANCES AND THE DANCERS

All of us delight in dancing and in beholding dances:
    Some of us desire a horse ballet
        Great and heavy horses,
Percherons with limbs like heavy but supple sandbags
    Dragging and lumbering in an *Alla Tedesca,*
        and then, at the horse show, the cavalry of Vienna,
        and then the sleek race horses of Saratoga:

All of us delight in the formal dancing of others
    Because we are bursting with the force of uncontrollable desire:
        Hence, where there are horses, as where there are rivers
and skaters—*Virtuosi* of the body's ebullience and deftness,
    By the spirit captured
        and trained to rapture.

Then there is a party of the city, the theatre and the school,
Then there is a dancing of the heart and the heart's birthday.
And even at the numbed peak of intensest winter cold
The skaters below the hill on the frozen lake or white courts,
Turn like the stars in free constellations

Under the blue; a cold shining, and seem more radiant and serene,
Than statues of the white goddess, Juno, the classic
        and imagined queen.

THE FAMOUS RESORT IN LATE AUTUMN

The shouting of the sea and the storm storming
Was loud and louder, loud enough to waken the rocks
     & to shock
The stilt-borne salt-burnt spray-pocked creaking
     boardwalk
Which looking upon the ever-freshness of the unresting
foaming erupting ocean as an ancient crippled
      and exhausted old man
      gazing from the shore
As if the day and the summer and the carnival were no more
But only & forever the low and leaden night
Of the senseless sea struggling with the awakened rocks.

HE WHO EXCUSES HIMSELF
ALSO ACCUSES HIMSELF

Listen, the dark lark chants once more
     Only the guilty are truly good!
A truth heartbreaking as war
     The penitent have understood.

Harken, how the daemon once more sings
     As once, of love, to Socrates,
Or blesses the blankness of the snow,
     Since white is all colors, in disguise.

The dark bird whispers: *Have you understood
How only the guilty can be truly good?*

WHEN I REMEMBER THE EVENT

When I remember the advent of the dazzling beauty
  As it descended, sudden and unknown,
I turn again to stiffened stone, alone
  With the poverty of having known the dazzling of beauty,
But only as a memory is known, only as a lake,
  A weekend or midnight
Know the glory streaming the great blue heights
  Riding in a storm of white disorder
  The cavalry of Aurora Borealis.

TO A FUGITIVE

The night you got away, I dreamed you rose
Out of the earth to lean on a young tree.
Then they were there, hulking the moon away,
The great dogs rooting, snuffing up the grass.
You raise a hand, hungry to hold your lips
Out of the waiting air; but lights begin
Spidering the ground; O they come closing in,
The beam searches your face like fingertips.

Hurry, Maguire, hammer the body down,
Crouch to the wall again, shackles the cold
Machine guns and the sheriff and the cars:
Divide the bright bars of the cornered bone,
Strip, run for it, break the last law, unfold,
Dart down the alley, race between the stars.

POEM

    . . . *window* . . . *winter* . . .
The winter woods are wire and black

And by a vivid death possessed:
The orchard trees describe a rack
Upon the snow's blank vacant breast.
                    . . . *a shroud, a cloud, a lunar myth* . . .
The trees' stripped lines writhe and arise
As in a Fury's passionate cry.
As if there were, beyond surprise,
A secret meaning in the sky!
                    Is there? There is!
                        Sure or perhaps?
                            Sure as perhaps.
The pulse of being is faint and low
As the grey cloth of the snow sky:
The scene is true as summer's show,
The woods of inter are a lie
                    true as most truths.

I REJOICE THAT THINGS ARE AS THEY ARE

I rejoice that things are as they are
And I rejoice in the blessed face
And renounce the voice
Because I cannot hope to turn again
Consequently I rejoice, having to construct
Something upon which to rejoice,

And pray to God to have mercy upon us
And I pray that I may forget
Those matters which with myself I too much
Discuss, too much explain.
Because I do not hope to turn again
Let these words answer
For what is done, not to be done again.
May the judgement not be too heavy upon us.

PRAISE IS TRADITIONAL AND APPROPRIATE

I loved the wood because I found in it
Mushrooms, berries, beetles, birds and other words,
Hedgehogs, squirrels, memories, quarrels, and the damp smell
Of dead leaves, and former lives.
                I reached the first barn
—where wheat was stored—halfway up the slope of the ravine
And saw her dancing, glancing twinkly eyes
Full of the hope and love which all thought mean,
And slate-green, slate-blue, blue or black like the sunrise
Skies, and in their variety and in their sheen
I thought that she was looking down at me
As if she understood past, present, and futurity.

SIX POEMS

VITTORIO SERENI

Translated by Edouard Roditi

THOSE THOUGHTS OF DISASTER THAT HAUNT YOU

and of catastrophe too
in that house where you
have come to live, already
inhabited by
the idea that you came
to die here
—and all those friendly people smiling at you
certainly this time
they all know you are dying and that's why
they smile at you

SECOND FRIGHT

It isn't at all alarmed
this voice that calls me
and calls me, only me,
from the street beneath my home

at one o'clock at night.
It's a brief awakening of the wind,
a fugitive shower of rain.
As it utters my name it refrains
from numbering my failures or reproaching me my past.
Very gently—Vittorio, Vittorio—
it disarms me, arms me,
arming myself against myself.

PROGRESS II

Some, I know, are not content
to wish me dead. That's what they hope,
to see me dead, but disgracefully too. They don't know
that I'm guilty of something even worse: I've
miniaturized them in my memory.

But those here are leaves,
nonsense and signs working on a huge scale,
not those congealed in miniature and who have nothing to do here
—and they would be right if they only knew it—
for all time shriveled up in the process of casting
and fossilized in the concrete as it sets.

I WAS TRANSLATING RENÉ CHAR

I.

In my own way, René Char,
and with my own means,
but with your materials.

In the day that glows splendidly above the gloaming
once it has crossed the threshold of its death-struggle

or else trembling after all those
dusty strides that raise
Spring behind them

Water has flowed, a hope
that one might drink all its greenery
under the Empire of Summer

II. *Muezzin*

From the highest tower
the refrain of ill omen
calls us to mend our ways
but from what faults, what further sins?

He says that Allah is great
and in this hour of the night
in this dead hour
I can well believe him.

III. *Lay Temple*

From the esplanades, very solemnly
among the stairways and colonnades
the trick perspective rises
towards the gnats of death.

How they become dappled with gold,
ready to light up an eternity
from one shore to the next,
and thus little by little in the spirit
the tyranny too and lastly
the destitution and betrayal.

SUNDAY AFTER THE WAR

For two who meet again on a Sunday
after the War,
can the desert wastes of the sea
still blossom again?

Love me, says he, returning,
Love me with all your strength and your might
so as to compensate for all those years,
but

in those first months of the War
when Sundays were only
mild despair, a dizziness
of bells and a residue
of smoke trailing behind
the last Amsterdam passenger ship. . . .

And they devour each other with their eyes,
seek each other, reach out with their hands
secretly towards each other over the linen tablecloth

. . . . lonely sea for so many years
that can be counted in waves,
stretch of sea now surprised
by time turned to stone in a space
of speechlessness. . . .
Can the sea's desert wastes blossom again?

Not only do they sniff at each other and watch each other,
both equally gentle and almost tender
—he's British and she's Flemish—
but suddenly they then begin to discuss it
today when it isn't even a Sunday.

ON A MOUNTAIN EXCURSION

"To sum it all up, existence doesn't exist,"
(but the other one replies: "go and read some poets
and they'll tell you
that although it's inexistent it yet exists").
This absurd dialogue continued over the hills
a couple of paths lower down
towards the sea,
are they making these speeches
at noon when the midsummer sun is at its hottest,
these kids, aren't they kids?—I wondered
as I shambled, dragging my feet among these stone quarries.

Finally, it's all meaningless
except for a few embittered passers-by
when for all time in their memory
whole fragments of nature impress themselves
and freeze in their gaze.
                        But it was I
who passed by, it was I,
perplexed but not really embittered.

SEVEN POEMS

JAMES L. WEIL

SEASCAPE—VIEW FROM OSSABOW

Pile two
unequal

rectangles

to equal
a third.

VIEW FROM THE BARN

Slide the door
and create

and cancel
rectangles.

WIND IN A CORNFIELD

Silvery
these stalks shine

shapes of it
back, it no

thing blowing
blackly on.

DOORS

Two mirrors bat
it back and forth

—the image of

the unwanted
infinitely.

An infinite
eight doors open

on each other.
We count it eight

because we count
only one man

and infinite
because of him.

PINOAK TREES

They repeat
diminish

distantly
echo each
other off

the valley
wall they tell

us of—not
shown, which is
the story.

UNDER THE GINKGO TREE

That we think
we can count
the ginkgo

leaves is what
he meant us
to think. Now

we need not
know. He has
known for us.

Nights we think
we know how
he did it.

ENDYMION

It is as
if each greek

link wants and
cannot, wants

on. We would
recur so

it is as
if we do.

NOTES ON CONTRIBUTORS

JOHN ALLMAN is the author of three books of poetry, including *Clio's Children* and *Scenarios for a Mixed Landscape*, both published by New Directions. "Biology" is taken from his collection of science poems, *Curve Away from Stillness*, forthcoming in 1988.

Editor of the literary magazine *Ambit* (London), MARTIN BAX practices medicine as a pediatrician as well as being Senior Research Fellow at Charing Cross Medical School and Senior Editor of *Developmental Medicine and Child Neurology*.

JOE DAVID BELLAMY lives in upstate New York and teaches at St. Lawrence University. His books include *Moral Fiction* (Fiction International), *The New Fiction* (interviews, from the University of Illinois Press), *Superfiction* (an anthology, from Random House), and a collection of poetry, *The Olympic Gold Medalist* (North American Review Press).

MACLIN BOCOCK's latest story appeared in the 1987 Centennial Issue of *Sequoia*. Another story was one of the winners of the Sixth PEN Syndicated Fiction Competition.

RICHARD M. BOMSTEIN's books are *For the Sake of Argument: American Poems* and *Footnoise: American Poems*. Last fall he created and produced The Muddy River Poetry Festival.

A 1987–88 Fulbright Fellow to Japan, ALAN M. BROWN recently completed his first novel, *Below the Equator*.

ANDREI CODRESCU's latest books are *A Craving for Swan* (essays, from Ohio State University Press) and *Comrade Past & Mr. Present* (poetry, from Coffee House Press). A professor of English at Louisiana State University in Baton Rouge, he is also an editor of *Exquisite Corpse* and a regular commentator on National Public Radio's *All Things Considered*.

PHILIPPE DENIS studied at the Sorbonne with Roland Barthes and Gaeten Picon, receiving his degree in 1973. The first of his three collections, *Cahier d'ombres,* won the celebrated Cino del Duca prize. This was followed by *Revif* and *Carnet d'un aveuglement.* Translator and poet CID CORMAN lives in Japan. His most recent books include *Aegis: Selected Poems* (Station Hill Press), *Root Song* (Potes & Poets Press), and *Tu* (Coffee House Press).

Born in Tokyo in 1823, SHUSAKU ENDO is one of Japan's leading novelists. He was baptized a Catholic as a child, and the inner conflict of a Japanese as Catholic is a recurring theme in his writing. His most recent book published in English is *The Samurai* (translated by Van C. Gessel, Harper & Row), a historical novel based on a Japanese mission to Europe and Mexico during the seventeenth century. LAWRENCE ROGERS teaches Japanese literature at the Hilo campus of the University of Hawaii. His translations have appeared in *Japan Quarterly, Translation,* and *Monumenta Nipponica.*

A second version of CLAYTON ESHLEMAN's "Children of the Monosyllable" appeared in *Sulfur* #19. His selected poems (*The Name Encanyoned River*) appeared in 1986; in 1988 MacPherson & Company will publish his selected prose; and Paragon Books will soon publish a selection of his translations, *Conductors of the Pit.* He currently teaches at Eastern Michigan University.

Editor of the *Olson-Corman Correspondence* (National Poetry Foundation) and author of *Nightvision* (poems, from Pig Press, London), GEORGE EVANS also created *Streetfare Journal,* a project of poetry posters for buses and subway cars nationwide.

GAVIN EWART's *Selected Poems 1933–1987* is forthcoming from New Directions. Born in London in 1916, Ewart was educated at Wellington College and Christ's College, Cambridge. After six years service in the British Army, he worked as a salesman in publishing, for the British Council, and as an advertising copywriter. Since 1971 he has been a freelance writer. A fellow of the Royal Society of Literature, he has received the Cholmondely Award for Poetry.

Assistant director of the Poetry Center at San Francisco State University, ROBERT GLÜCK's two most recent books are a novel, *Jack the Modernist* (Seahorse) and a collection of stories, *Elements of a Coffee Service* (Four Seasons Foundation).

JAMES B. HALL is a short-story writer whose third collection, *The Short Hall*, will appear soon in a paperback edition. He lives in Santa Cruz, California.

New Directions has recently published *Nights* by H. D. (1886–1961). Written under the pseudonym of John Helforth, the novel was originally printed privately in a limited edition of one hundred copies in the 1930s—a self-portrait from H. D.'s "hidden" years. "Two Americans" was privately printed in 1930.

EDWIN HONIG, Professor Emeritus of English and American Literature at Brown University, was knighted in honor of his recently published Fernando Pessoa translations by the Socialist president of Portugal.

JAMES LAUGHLIN's recent books include *Stolen and Contaminated Poems* (Turkey Press), *Selected Poems, 1935–1985* (City Lights), *The House of Light* (Grenfell Press), and *The Owl of Minerva* (Copper Canyon Press). *Ez as Wuz*, essays on Ezra Pound, will soon appear from Graywolf Press.

THOMAS PARKINSON is a professor of English at the University of California, Berkeley. His latest book is a collection of essays, *Poets, Poems, Movements* (UMI Research Press).

CATHERINE PETROSKI teaches at Duke University and is the author of *Gravity & Other Stories* (Fiction International).

The newest volume in New Directions' ongoing series, The Correspondence of EZRA POUND, is *Pound/Zukofsky*, edited by Barry Ahearn. Scheduled for 1988 is *Pound/Little Review*. DONALD GALLUP, who prepared the text of "The Consolations of Matrimony," is the author of the definitive *Ezra Pound: A Bibliography* (The University Press of Virginia).

The Italian poet VITTORIO SERENI (1913–83) was born in Luino. Teaching at a secondary school when World War II broke out, he was captured by the Americans and spent over two years in a prison camp in Africa. There he wrote the poems that formed his first book, *Diario d'Algeria*. After 1968 he was an editor at Mondadori, in Milan, in charge of *L'Almanaco dello Specchio*. Selections of Sereni's poems also appeared in *ND27, ND37, ND47,* and *Sixteen Poems* is available from Red Dust. An American long resident in Paris, EDOUARD RODITI is an internationally known linguist, scholar, art critic, translator, and author. Last year New Directions published his updated study, *Oscar Wilde*.

The Ego Is Always at the Wheel, a collection of short humorous essays by DELMORE SCHWARTZ (1913–66), was recently published by New Directions. Many of these bagatelles were only recently discovered among the poet's papers at Yale by ROBERT PHILLIPS, poet, editor, and literary executor for the Estate of Delmore Schwartz.

JAMES L. WEIL is the publisher of the Elizabeth Press. Warwick Press will issue his new collection of poems, *Jacques' Geometry,* in 1988.